Why couldn't ~~clumsy, pas~~ ~~ding?~~

As this half-amused, half-irritated thought passed through Rosalie's mind, their eyes locked once more and suddenly her dispassionate assessment of Daniel's looks and personality ignited into a moment of such unexpected sensual awareness that she caught her breath.

She suddenly understood the mystery ingredient in that frank, persistent gaze. He was attracted to her and didn't mind letting her see it. In fact, he *wanted* her to see it.

Dear Reader

This month we offer you Accident and Emergency, Cardiac, Physiotherapy, and a holiday resort in Egypt — how's that for variety? Lynne Collins gives us a hero who is dogged by gossip, Lilian Darcy an older heroine coping with passion for a younger man, Drusilla Douglas a heroine confused by identical twins, and Margaret Barker gives us a pair who had met before. . .

We hope you enjoy learning how they solve their problems!

The Editor

Lilian Darcy is Australian, but on her marriage made her home in America. She writes for theatre, film and television, as well as romantic fiction, and she likes winter sports, music, travel and the study of languages. Hospital volunteer work and friends in the medical profession provide the research background for her novels; she enjoys being able to create realistic modern stories, believable characters, and a romance that will stand the test of time.

Recent titles by the same author:

A PRIVATE ARRANGEMENT
THE BECKHILL TRADITION

HEART CALL

BY

LILIAN DARCY

MILLS & BOON LIMITED
ETON HOUSE   18–24 PARADISE ROAD
RICHMOND   SURREY   TW9 1SR

First published in Great Britain 1993 by Mills & Boon Limited

© Lilian Darcy 1993

Australian copyright 1993 Philippine copyright 1993 This edition 1993

ISBN 0 263 78343 X

Set in 10 on 10½ pt Linotron Times 03-9309-60104

Typeset in Great Britain by Centracet, Cambridge Made and printed in Great Britain

CHAPTER ONE

ROSALIE CRANE put down her well-worn trowel, flung sturdy leather gardening gloves on to a lichen-encrusted rock and stretched her back. There was time for another hour or more in her beloved garden before she had to start thinking about lunch and getting ready for work, but somehow she just didn't feel like it.

It was a glorious day, too, the kind that she usually loved to spend among the charmingly haphazard layout of flowerbeds, rockeries, herb plantings and rows of vegetables. White balls of cloud drifted in a blue sky like lazily grazing sheep, and a mild May breeze blew the coconut scent of gorse across to Rosalie from the rolling open lands that led to the cliff-tops a mile away.

Perhaps I should experiment with something new in the garden this year. . .she thought vaguely. A planting of hardy cyclamens. . .or a little bonsai pavilion. She felt an immediate urge to dash off to an exotic plant nursery and buy a dozen untried specimens, but then decided sensibly, No, I should do my homework first, find out what's involved. Then I can jump in whole-heartedly and not make a mess of it.

She wandered down the path that led to the little fish-pond she had put in one summer several years ago and watched the lazy goldfish slipping beneath the rounded water-lily pads, then wandered back again to the tray of alyssum. One tray was already planted in the rockery, so that soon a fragrant carpet of white and purple would spill all over the place. This second tray. . .

I don't think I'll do it today. I'll go for a walk along the cliffs instead.

This decided, she scarcely had the patience to put
away her tools and change out of the earth-stained
denim overalls she always wore in the garden. After
climbing into tartan trousers and flinging a cream
cotton pullover over her head, she grabbed an apple
from the glossy wooden bowl on the sideboard and
was off, not locking the stone cottage, not picking up
a scarf, not taking her purse in case she remembered
an errand to do in the village on her way home.

It was windy along the cliffs and the sea was a dark,
fresh blue, shading to green as it shelved up to the
shingle beach and changing abruptly to white as it
crashed on the rocks below Rosalie's feet. Her full-
bodied, below-shoulder-length hair blew wildly and it
felt glorious. The silky auburn-red strands would need
a thorough taming before she assumed the role of ward
sister on the Kilborne Cardiac Ward at St Bede's
Hospital, just outside Plymouth, this afternoon, but
she didn't care. Somehow, the buffeting sea breeze
with its strong flavour of salt was necessary to her
today to knock this restlessness out of her.

It wasn't the first time this spring that the feeling
had come over her and she trod the cliff path unthink-
ingly as she tried to work out what the problem was.

Was it a problem? She didn't even know that. The
matter certainly did demand some thought, then.
Could it be Howard Trevalley? He had first asked her
out nearly a year ago now, and two weeks ago, for the
first time, he had said something that suggested his
slow and very discreet courtship might be heading
somewhere.

'This is very pleasant, my dear, isn't it?' He was
leaning back in his chair after a filling meal. They were
at Baldwin's, the restaurant he almost always chose, at
their usual secluded table. He never referred to the
fact that they had this table, but Rosalie was under no
illusions about the reason for his insistence on it. He

didn't want to risk anyone from the hospital seeing them here together.

'Mm, it is very pleasant,' she had agreed gently.

As the hospital's senior cardiac surgeon, Howard Trevalley was necessarily an experienced and intelligent man. The conversation they had had together this evening had been interesting, if, as it always was, rather safe and predictable. The food had been nice, too. . .as it always was. Baldwin's offered plain fare such as steak or roast, with never the hint of an unexpected seasoning. By this time, Rosalie had tried almost everything on the menu more than once.

'I'd been wondering,' the fifty-three-year-old widower said now, 'if you'd like to try a weekend away together soon?' He added hastily. 'We'd have our own rooms, of course. I'm a light sleeper, and——' He broke off, realising that he had got himself on to an unfortunate side-track. Recovering his equilibrium somewhat, he continued, 'It's a big step in. . .in. . . Well, do give yourself some time to think. No need to rush. Perhaps in August. We could fly up to Scotland, hire a car and do some motoring. Or Wales, perhaps.'

'Yes, that sounds lovely. As you said, I will think about it. Perhaps closer to the time, we might both know——'

'Exactly, exactly,' he came in over her, and she wondered as she studied the solemn face that had reddened down to his neck if he was sorry he had made such a dramatic suggestion, separate rooms notwithstanding.

He had made no demands on her physically during the time they had spent together. His courteous kisses were warm and not unpleasant, however, and in a way it would be easier if their relationship moved to a more passionate footing, especially while they were in the safety of new surroundings.

'Do I want to go to Scotland with him?' Rosalie asked the wind on the cliffs.

She felt that it would be good if she did. She *wanted* to want to go. She wished he hadn't suggested Scotland, though, and hoped she would be able to steer him towards Wales. . .if the plan came to anything. Scotland was where she had spent her honeymoon, and that had been in August, too. My goodness, it was nearly nineteen years ago! Rosalie had been eighteen then. She was thirty-seven now.

And it was nearly fifteen years since Mike's sudden death from asthma one unseasonably oppressive September night. Rosalie shook her shoulders and quickened her pace along the cliff-top. Mike would have been forty-nine by now, had he lived—nearly as old as Howard. They were men of the same generation, both born during the war, and this fact gave her an added sense of comfort and security.

'If I want to marry again. . .' and she knew that most women in her position would jump at the opportunity '. . . Howard is an ideal choice. I'm very lucky.'

She said the words very firmly aloud, and a lad on a touring bicycle pedalling past her at a dangerous pace looked at her as if she were mad—a wild-haired woman with wind-buffeted pink cheeks talking to herself up here on the cliff. She laughed briefly, and if he had heard that he probably thought that she was madder still.

I'm very lucky. The words repeated themselves in her head and she sensibly added up all the reasons why this was so. Howard was well-off, successful, kind. He already had a son and a daughter from his first marriage, so it wouldn't matter. . .about children.

Rosalie felt a stab of acute pain and disappointment ambush her unexpectedly out of the past. Although she had married young, she had wanted children straight away. Mike was thirty at the time and he was ready, too, so they took no precautions and were laughingly expectant of conceiving almost immediately.

'We'll have twins,' Mike had said teasingly, 'then six more!'

But it hadn't happened. A year had passed, and Rosalie had wanted to talk to the doctor about it.

'Let's wait,' was Mike's decision. Despite his lifelong battle with asthma, or perhaps because of it, he had always been very reluctant to consult a medical professional. 'You're young. Your hormones probably haven't settled down into the proper rhythm yet.'

At the time, knowing nothing about medicine or physiology herself, Rosalie had accepted this idea, and they had gone on trying with hopes scarcely dampened. Two more years had passed, and for Rosalie they had been increasingly unhappy ones. Not wanting to worry Mike, or to seem obsessive, she had begun keeping her feelings more and more to herself, which had only made them grow stronger.

'Relax,' was Mike's answer on the rare occasions when she did say something. 'That happens all the time, I'm told. If a woman really wants too hard to get pregnant, she tightens up somehow and the anxiety stops it from happening.'

For another year, Rosalie had accepted this, too, but finally, one miserably wet and cold July day fifteen years ago, she had unleashed her carefully controlled and hidden feelings, and, after a stormy row and a flood of tears, Mike had agreed that they ought to seek professional help. The specialist had been wonderful, although Rosalie could still remember the fleeting betrayal of pity in his face when she told him that they had been trying for four years.

He must know already that nothing can be done, she had thought miserably then, and, although she now knew that often much *could* be done, this first impression had stayed with her so that she felt down to the marrow of her bones that she would never be able to bear a child.

'We'll start some simple tests at your next appointment,' Dr Huxtable had said, but Rosalie hadn't been able to keep her next appointment. Mike's funeral had taken place the same day.

Rosalie came to a halt where the cliff path branched towards a sharp promontory in one direction and down to a second shingled beach in the other. She took the fork that led to the promontory. It was only fifty yards. She needed to watch those crashing waves below for a few precious minutes, then it was time to head back.

Thoughts of Mike's death were not truly painful any more. Time had softened the sharpness of her initial agony, and the only thing that she now regretted was that her desire for a child had eaten away at so much of the happiness of their time together. Whenever she thought of a disagreement they had had, or a distance between them, she could always put it down to her own feelings. If only they had sought professional help sooner!

In the weeks following Mike's death, and without blaming him for letting the matter drift for so long, this was the thought that kept recurring in her, and, as her financial affairs were settled and questions about the future began to loom, the turmoil of regret crystallised into a determination to study nursing so that she could help other people who were similarly handicapped by fear or ignorance about medical matters.

And so here she was today, not working in obstetrics as she had at first planned to do. Being among all those precious babies and happy parents had hurt her too much at first. It didn't hurt now. She was contented and comfortable in her life and had long since grown accustomed to her childless state, and to life as a hardworking widow. Chance had led her early in her training to a cardiac ward, and as she qualified and experienced other areas of nursing her interest in cardiac care had stayed and grown so that now it was her speciality and she couldn't imagine working anywhere else.

Nor could she imagine living anywhere other than the old but comfortably modernised stone cottage Mike had left to her, with its sheltered, rambling garden and secluded position tucked away in the tiny Devon village of Torbury Bay just a minute's walk from the sea. She liked her life, her work, her routine, and if it had been feeling just a little too staid and comfortable and unchanging of late, well, Howard Trevalley's increasing attentions would surely provide some sort of a fillip.

Howard. . . That *must* be why she was feeling so restless today, and so open to memories of the past. Turning from the cliff at last, she walked briskly back along the path, realising only now that the clouds were thickening in the sky and she had been out for quite some time.

Quite some time, indeed! It was two by the kitchen clock and she had to bolt down a ham and salad sandwich, a pear and a piece of lemon cake without her habitual leisurely cup of tea as she read the newspaper.

Standing before the long mirror in her bright bedroom, Rosalie assessed the damage the wind had done to her hair and realised that the tangles would take far more combing than she had time for. Instead, she was forced to content herself with a vigorous brushing before twisting the rich rusty fullness into a knot at the back of her head and fastening it with pins. Fortunately, the effect was not nearly as disastrous as she had feared at first. The half-tamed tangles added to the slight springiness of her hair's natural wave so that the abundant red mass fluffed out to frame her face in a glossy halo.

Rosalie Crane had unusual colouring for a redhead. Her eyes were brown, not blue or green, her brows were dark and her skin, although very fair so that when she had been out in the open, like this morning, her cheeks went a glowing pink, was unmarked by

freckles or coarseness. This colouring meant that,
unlike most redheads, she could get away with wearing
pink, and when she did so the effect was daring and
dramatic.

Less daring, but none the less quite flattering to
both her colouring and her figure, was the dark blue
uniform of a ward sister that she slipped into now. A
black belt with silver buckle, semi-transparent black
tights, comfortable black leather shoes, a quick sketch
of colourless lipgloss on her wide mouth and she was
ready. . .

And only just in time.

'Sister, what do you think? *Is* Mr Giles a candidate for
surgery?'

It was Howard Trevalley who spoke, and his face
and voice openly telegraphed impatience. Rosalie
flushed. She couldn't blame him for being angry, and
she couldn't expect him to soften his anger just because
they were personally involved—especially since no one
else on the staff knew about it.

In fact, she *hadn't* been on time when she arrived on
the ward. She had been five minutes late—very
unusual for her, and she couldn't have picked a worse
day to do it on. The new registrar in Cardiology,
Daniel Canaday, had started yesterday, which had
been her day off, and she should have been here early
today so that Howard could introduce her to the man.
He had mentioned on Friday that he wanted to.
Meanwhile, of course, Dr Max Hillston, director of
the Division of Cardiology, had decreed that there
would be a ward conference at three, attended by both
the incoming and outgoing ward sister, as well as Mr
Trevalley, Dr Canaday, and several junior physicians,
surgeons and medical students into the bargain.

Rosalie had catapulted breathlessly into the middle
of this confusion, feeling like a schoolgirl late to
lessons, had spent ten minutes recovering her pro-

fessional composure and gathering her wits, and was now understandably expected to have something useful to contribute. She forced herself to think about Arthur Giles.

'Well, he's very keen to have the surgery,' she began, then stopped. Someone was staring at her across the small, crowded space. An unfamiliar face, but not a medical student, surely. He looked too assured for that. It must be Dr Canaday, she realised, and his unbroken scrutiny was very unnerving. What on earth did he mean by it? Rallying herself, she managed to continue. '*Extremely* keen.' There was a rumble from Howard Trevalley's throat that seemed to be saying, So what's the problem?

'In fact. . .' The word came out of her as a snap. Her eyes met those of Dr Canaday and she found that they were very black and unfathomable. Then at last he looked away. 'I'd say he's almost too keen. He talks about a double bypass as if it's a "cure" and although we've tried to explain to him that he'll still have heart-disease it doesn't seem to be getting through.'

She remembered how he had waved away more than one explanation about how the new arterial vessels, which literally bypassed the old, clogged sites and were made from veins grafted from his legs or chest, would clog in time as surely as his original arteries had done, if he kept to his previous diet and routine.

'Yes, he's not responsive to the idea of lifestyle changes at all,' Sister Megan Blair came in. She sat on the edge of the most uncomfortable chair in the room, and was obviously anxious for her part in this session to be over so that she could collect her two children from school on time.

'He wants us to do the surgery then send him home, problem solved,' Rosalie went on.

'Then surely that's an attitude problem that can be addressed after the surgery,' Howard said.

'Oh, my objection isn't to surgery as such,' Dr
Canaday came in.

So the new man was putting spanners in the works
already, Rosalie noted. *And* he was looking at her
again. She flushed more deeply. What was wrong with
him? Or with her? She couldn't read his expression. It
wasn't hostile. It was certainly curious, if she judged
correctly, but there was something more. As the
wrangle over Mr Giles continued, began to include the
students, and turned into the ongoing and unresolvable
debate about the merits of medicine over surgery,
Rosalie allowed herself to study the new cardiologist.

He was younger than she had expected. He looked
to be in his early thirties, and she had heard about his
recent two years at the Cleveland Clinic in the United
States — one of the most famous and prestigious cardiac centres in the world. The opportunity of working
there wasn't given to just any aspiring heart specialist,
so he must have brains, ambition and ability.

He was extremely good-looking, too, she realised
with a sinking heart. She could already think of three
of her younger nurses who would be swooning over
him within a week — swooning over that wavy dark
brown hair, so dark it was almost black, and those
black eyes fringed with such thick lashes. What a
nuisance it would be! She could see an intensity and
dynamism in him, too, that would attract the junior
nurses more surely even than those devastating looks.
Why couldn't the man have been clumsy, pasty-faced
and balding?

Then, as this half-amused, half-irritated thought
passed through her mind, their eyes locked once more
and suddenly her dispassionate assessment of his looks
and personality ignited into a moment of such unexpected sensual awareness that she caught her breath,
felt her heart in her throat and had to stare down at
the forest-green carpet to regain control.

The worst thing about it was her realisation of what

had caused that sudden change in her perception. It was the way he was looking at her. She suddenly understood the mystery ingredient in that frank, persistent gaze. He was attracted to her and didn't mind letting her see it. In fact, he *wanted* her to see it. He had wanted that sudden sizzling locking of their gaze, and now as she dared to look up again she found that a lazy, satisfied and rather private smile was playing on his sensitively drawn lips.

He knows that I responded, that I felt it too, she thought confusedly. It's ridiculous! Awful!

Her heart was pounding now, her palms were damp, and her mind boiled with helpless thoughts like the sea boiling in the wake of a powerful boat. With an immense effort, she brought her focus back to the medical discussion and so, evidently, did Daniel Canaday.

'Angioplasty,' he said suddenly.

Rosalie, who had not heard a word of the previous three minutes of talk, started slightly, but nobody noticed, thank goodness, and nobody else seemed surprised at Dr Canaday's abrupt re-entry into the director's curt question as to what immediate action he did propose in Arthur Giles's case.

'Angioplasty. . .' Howard said thoughtfully. 'Yes, there's certainly justification for it on medical grounds. The two blockages are in the right spot. But how will it help with the man's attitude problem?'

'It may not,' Dr Canaday admitted cheerfully but seriously. 'It buys us some time, though. He's a young man. Thirty-seven. If he has the bypass now and does nothing to change his lifestyle, those new grafted vessels are going to be clogged themselves before he's fifty. An angioplasty can postpone the need for bypass. Meanwhile, his own doctor can work on getting through to him about smoking, stress. . .'

'Yes, all right, you've convinced me,' Howard

Trevalley conceded abruptly. 'You'd like to do it yourself, I presume?'

'Yes. I have a batch of them scheduled for tomorrow.'

Although technically an invasive procedure, the insertion of a balloon catheter into the affected vessels, to literally press the clogging material back against the vessel walls, was a fairly simple matter these days, done under local anaesthetic and not qualifying as surgery.

'Good. That'll free up a bed for us far more quickly, too,' Max Hillston commented.

One of the students ventured to ask a question, it was quickly answered by Mr Trevalley and the conference moved on, covering several more problematic cases in as many minutes. A relieved Sister Blair was finally on her way at half-past three, the doctors departed for a round in Cardiac Intensive Care, and Rosalie took charge of her ward.

It was a step down in level of care from the CICU, where patients went immediately following surgery or when in acute danger of heart failure. There, the ratio of staff to patients was one to two, or even better, while here it was approximately one to four, with twenty-seven beds and eight nursing staff, as well as a junior student on rotation from time to time. A nurse had to be highly qualified and trained to work here, and in return was permitted to do some tasks that on other wards were usually only done by doctors.

By half-past six that evening, Rosalie had forgotten all about Daniel Canaday. She decided to snatch half an hour for her meal, leaving the ward in the capable hands of Margaret Binns, a likeable girl in her late twenties who was soon to leave St Bede's to get married and take up a position as ward sister in a cardiac unit in Bath. Margaret and some of the other nurses had already eaten, but Rosalie was accompanied by two juniors whom she had directed to take the second meal break as she was doing.

The dining-room was quiet by this time. Rosalie took carrot soup, chicken and vegetable risotto, a wholemeal bread roll and fruit salad, and went to her usual corner by the window. The juniors did not join her nor invite her to join them, and she wasn't surprised or disappointed. She preferred to eat alone or with colleagues at her own level, reasoning that the younger girls didn't need her dampening effect on their often very frivolous and irreverent conversation. None of her particular cronies was around this evening, she found, so she settled at her table, happily alone.

Alone, that was until a voice startled her into looking up from the novel she was reading and the last mouthfuls of her soup, and she found that the new cardiologist was standing there with a full tray. 'May I join you?'

'Of course,' she murmured, her heart thumping ridiculously.

If only she had seen him coming so that she could have prepared herself a little! But why prepare herself? She must not let that tumultuous moment this afternoon loom over her like this. In fact, judging by his blandly friendly manner towards her now, she might well have imagined the whole thing.

'Sit down,' she added carefully, and he did so.

'Thanks for supporting me this afternoon over Arthur Giles,' he said.

'Yes,' she nodded. 'It seems we both reached the same conclusion about his eagerness for the operation.'

'And I think it was you that convinced Trevalley, not me,' the cardiologist said generously. 'He seems to trust his nurses, which is nice.'

'Yes, he's very good that way,' she agreed neutrally, aware, as she always was these days, of the private

friendship she shared with the senior cardiac surgeon.
She felt confident, though, that no one ever suspected
this friendship when she spoke about Howard
Trevalley. Dr Canaday certainly didn't look curious or
suspicious now.

'How's the risotto?' he asked, after a silence during
which he took a gulp of the tomato juice on his tray.

'Quite good, actually.'

'Yes, it looks better than this steak and kidney, I
must say.'

'Oh, the steak and kidney. . .!' she laughed, with a
light-hearted lift of her neat chin.

'Notorious, is it?' he grinned back.

'To old-timers like me, yes.'

'You'll have to give me some tips, then, on what to
choose.'

'It's fairly simple, really. Just order whatever is in
shortest supply. Word gets round fast about the pick
of the day.'

He laughed now, too, and she decided that she
really *must* have imagined this afternoon—although
that in itself was a little disturbing, since she wasn't
usually given to fantasies of that kind, especially about
younger men.

Relaxing at last as they ate together, she was able to
conclude very quickly—surprisingly so, perhaps—that
she liked the new cardiologist. He wasn't as arrogant
and impatient as she had expected, considering his
recent return from the Cleveland Clinic. Several years
ago, there had been another cardiologist fresh from a
stint at that illustrious institute, and he had peppered
every second sentence with the phrase, 'At Cleveland,
we. . .' until she wanted to scream. To everyone's
relief—and particularly to her own, since he had asked
her out several times and she didn't like him at all—
the man had moved on after two years.

Daniel Canaday, though, was different. 'I'm surprised to find you here so late,' she said to him, 'when you've only just started the job.'

'But that's precisely when I *should* be staying late. Getting to know the ropes. For example. . .what can you tell me about this heart care project that's being mooted?'

The sudden question took her by surprise a little. The idea of a community outreach campaign to increase public awareness about heart-disease and its prevention had been knocking around for several months now, but it hadn't got very far as yet and Rosalie was of the private opinion that it possibly never would. Everyone was very enthusiastic in theory, pointing to similar programmes that had been a success elsewhere, but no one seemed prepared to take on the burden of strong leadership, especially since it was known that at the moment there was only the tiniest trickle of funds available. The hospital's new heart transplant programme seemed to be swallowing everyone's time and energy. This was necessary and understandable, but it was also true, Rosalie was cynically aware, that transplant surgery was far more glamorous and prestigious than a programme of grassroots public education. But, since she was reluctant to present this rather sceptical viewpoint to a near-stranger, her response to Dr Canaday was very bland and distinctly unhelpful.

'I can't tell you very much,' she said to him with a camouflaging smile. 'There's not much to tell. It's a marvellous idea, of course, but——'

'Oh, yes, it's a marvellous idea,' he parroted with a sardonic grin and an impatient shift of his capable shoulders. 'Everyone agrees about that. Dr Whiffenpoof would get the thing organised if only he wasn't in some kind of fierce competition over status with Dr Poofenwhiff, and Dr Sputterchops would be tireless in his efforts if someone could guarantee that it would get him a top job in London five years down

the track, and Dr Musn'tgrumble would muck in with
an idea or two only he's too busy doing private
research into scalp treatments to try and save his
receding hairline, and. . .'

Rosalie battled against a spurt of laughter, lost the
battle, and decided to enjoy the moment. 'My goodness!' she managed to exclaim after a helpless minute
or two. A smile tickling one corner of his sensitive
mouth told her that he was pleased at her amused
response. 'How do you know all that about this place
in two days?'

He was exaggerating hugely, of course, but there
was a grain of truth in each of his caricatures, which
she had had no trouble in recognising despite the
outrageous names. He was right, too, in what his
words had implied. It was only the quirks of personality at the hospital that prevented the heart care
project from getting off the ground.

'I like to do my homework,' was his mild reply to
her exclamation.

The words struck a chord and Rosalie remembered
that she had thought the same thing just this afternoon
about her garden plans. 'Do your homework, then you
can jump in with both feet and not make a mess,' she
murmured, half to herself.

'Exactly,' was his deceptively lazy answer. 'And now
. . .tell me about how your ward gets on with Casualty.
Any problems there?'

'Wait a minute!' She could see that it would be all
too easy to give away too much to this man.

He seemed to sense the reason for her reluctance
and came in quickly, 'I'm not asking for gossip or
back-stabbing, just any ideas you've got about how
things could work more smoothly. And, more importantly, any suggestions for me, since I'm new. Don't
forget I've been working under a different system for
two years. Don't let me get away with anything that
makes life harder for you!'

His energy drew her in almost magnetically, and she found that he was right. There *were* things she needed to say to him and he listened with respect and interest. After several minutes of this, a silence fell between them and she found herself blurting what was in her head without stopping to wonder whether it was an appropriate comment to a near-stranger. 'It's obvious you've chosen the right profession, isn't it?'

He laughed, and didn't seem to resent the observation, then leaned forward to pick up a large cup of coffee, saying, 'Yes, although I came very close to *not* choosing it.'

'That's hard to believe.' Without realising it, she had leaned forward a little too, so that this small table in the brightly lit cafeteria had acquired an odd sort of intimacy. 'You weren't planning to become a plumber at any stage, surely!'

'No, it wasn't that I'd decided to be something else, but I did decide very forcefully *not* to be a doctor.' And somehow she found that he was telling her the whole story while she listened with her elbow resting in the pool of fluorescent light on the table and her hand cupping her chin. 'My father was an orthopaedic surgeon, you see, and always encouraged me to think I'd be one, too. Then, in my first year of medicine, he had a massive heart attack and died several days later. . .'

Rosalie nodded as he talked, silently sympathetic, but did not waste words in some conventional expression of regret. She sensed that he wasn't asking for that.

'The whole experience was so brutal, I just chucked medicine altogether for the rest of the term. It seemed crazy. Here was Dad, a Harley Street specialist and he'd dropped in his tracks at forty-nine.' He looked up at her with a rueful grin. 'Those feelings don't make any sense at all, do they?'

'Oh, but I think they do,' Rosalie assured him gently.

'Well, all summer I wrestled with the thing and finally realised that I *did* want to do medicine, but not orthopaedics. That just didn't seem relevant any more. I wanted to stop people dying the way my father had died, so I managed to make up the work I'd missed, take some supplementary exams and get back into it.'

He made it sound simple, but Rosalie guessed it had not been. 'And how did your mother manage?' she asked gently now.

He stared down at his hands, then met her gaze steadily. 'She was crushed for a while, especially by the dreadful *paperwork* that death seems to create these days, getting finances straight and all that. Now, she's doing well. It was more than, oh, twelve years ago that it happened. She runs a rather successful interior design and furnishing business these days.'

'Sounds interesting.'

'It is. In fact, for the next few months she and my sister are based in Paris, setting up a branch there, which my sister will run. Amanda has an amazing flair for design, and an uncanny eye for what's really unusual.'

'So both of you are following in your respective parent's footsteps?' Rosalie said. The pride in his voice when he talked about his sister's talent was quite open.

'I guess we are,' he smiled.

Their eyes met disconcertingly for a moment, then her gaze faltered before his. She felt an unusual desire to match the personal revelations he had made to her with a story of her own, and said quietly. 'It's funny. . .my own impetus to go into nursing came from a personal experience of loss. . .'

'I imagine that's a fairly common story,' he responded seriously. 'It's a powerful motivating force.'

'Yes, that's true. . . Oh, heavens, is that the time?'

Curious to hear Sister Crane's own story, Daniel

Canaday was disappointed to see that she had caught sight of the fob-watch pinned to her dark blue uniform. She rose hastily and, with instinctive politeness, he did too. 'It was good to talk to you,' he said.

She nodded quickly, picked up her tray with its empty dishes and was off, her smoothly rounded hips swinging rhythmically in her haste to deposit the tray at the counter and return to the ward.

Daniel sat back to finish his coffee. On second thoughts, it was probably a good thing that she hadn't had time to tell the story of her own entry into the world of medicine. He had sensed that it was going to be even more personal than his own, and realised that she might well regret opening herself to a near-stranger so completely. In fact. . . He shook his head a little, suddenly bemused at how quickly the two of them had gone beyond trivialities this evening. He certainly hadn't intended it. All that stuff about his father. . .

Seeking Sister Crane out, here in the cafeteria, on the other hand, *had* been intentional. Her effect on his senses had been immediate, back in the ward conference, and he had seen no sense in pretending to himself that it was unimportant and would pass. Knowing himself to be a man of quick and decisive action, he had learned by now to let himself follow what almost amounted to an intuition about certain facets of his life. He had only regretted this trait in himself a handful of times, when it had not been sure-handed decisiveness born of self-knowledge, but rash impulse. . .the purchase of a second-hand motorbike at a fiendishly inflated price at the age of nineteen sprang to mind. . .and he couldn't see that he was going to regret following this thing with Sister Crane a little further.

If she turned out to be as fascinating as she looked, he would find out if she was unattached and ask her out. If, on the other hand, his first overwhelming

impression was not borne out, he would have had a
nice chat about the hospital and no harm done.

This was how his thoughts had gone *before* dinner.
Now, after a conversation that had gone considerably
deeper than the casual chat he had envisaged, he
already found it was more complicated than that. For
a start, his intuition was really making strong signals
over this. It had done so in Cleveland two years ago
when he first arrived there, and that had resulted in a
very satisfactory relationship with Dr Sharon Jantz.
Just emerging from a bitter and painful divorce,
though, Sharon hadn't wanted a serious commitment,
and neither had he. With Rosalie Crane, however, he
already sensed that it might be possible to get involved
far more deeply.

On the other hand, of course, he reminded himself
hastily, it was more than probable that she was already
involved with someone else. With the ripe, warm
beauty that had caught so powerfully at his own senses,
he found it hard to believe that her social life was
empty. She wore no wedding-ring, but that was the
only clue he had. . .

Daniel finished his coffee, stretched his capable
shoulders and rose, already impatient to follow things
through. He hated half-heartedness and uncertainty.
Even more, he hated pretence and prevarication. He
hoped that Rosalie Crane felt the same way.

Rosalie, on her way back to the ward, was also
thinking about her dinner-time interlude. He's nice,
she decided. Friendly, intelligent. . . Well and good.
Her dramatic reaction to his persistent gaze that afternoon now seemed quite ridiculous to her. He had been
assessing a future colleague. It was simply that, and it
was a relief to realise it. After all, she was thirty-seven,
and described herself quite contentedly as middle-
aged. He was thirty-two, she had discovered over
dinner, an age which, in a man — particularly a professional man — was the very prime of life.

No, her earlier concern that she would have several love-struck juniors on her hands was the accurate response to the advent of Daniel Canaday, and if he did create romantic havoc on her ward it would be with one of the fresh-faced, slender-figured blondes under her charge, *not* with herself. The idea was simply impossible. . . None the less, he was certainly going to be a stimulating and demanding colleague on the professional level!

Satisfied with this prognosis, Rosalie took the lift to the seventh floor, but then her own romantic prospects loomed at her, as she stepped out into the foyer, in the form of Howard Trevalley.

'I've been waiting for you to get back from dinner,' he said in a slightly aggrieved tone, and when Rosalie glanced at the fob-watch pinned to her uniform she saw that she had overstayed the half-hour she had promised to Margaret Binns.

'Sorry.' She frowned up at him.

Howard was tall, and beginning to stoop slightly. Some old photos he had showed her once had revealed him to be a very dashing man in his first youth, and he was still handsome, with thick pepper-and-salt hair, piercing blue eyes and a craggy though too long nose. His wife had died two years ago, and his first bewildered grief had changed gradually into a peevishness and irritability about the world in general that Rosalie felt she understood and frequently tried to soothe away.

'Did you want something in particular?' she asked now, touching him gently on the arm. No one could see them at present, although she could hear the sound of voices coming through the open door to the ward.

'Yes, to check that Friday is still all right with you. We haven't had a chance to talk this week.'

'Friday is fine,' she soothed. 'You know that's our regular day, and I keep it free now, as long as I'm not

working. I'd have let you know if anything else had
come up.'

'Of course you would. I'm sorry. I'll pick you up as
usual, then, and we'll go to Baldwin's, shall we?'

'It sounds lovely.'

He craned his head towards the door and glanced
quickly into the ward, saw that no one could see them
and that no one was approaching along the corridor,
then bent and kissed her, a swift, tender touch that
moved her but did not set her on fire. She had had no
expectation that it would. Even her response to Mike
had not been all that strong, and she had decided
during her marriage that passion came very low on her
list of necessary ingredients in a successful
relationship.

She was about to draw her face away from him when
suddenly she wanted more from the moment, and,
taking him by surprise, she reached up to rest slender
fingers on the fine woollen weave of his suit's grey
shoulders and kissed him with a restless eagerness she
had not shown to him before. Taken by surprise, he
responded, then buried his face in her rich hair. A
moment later, there was a soft, sighing clack, and the
lift doors opened just yards from where they stood, to
reveal Daniel Canday.

The way they sprang apart and each stared guiltily
at the floor while Howard essayed a gruff greeting
probably gave away the secret of their private romance
more effectively than if they had remained entwined.
Their embrace could have been one of friendship or
comfort, but their guilty distance now proved that it
was not. It seemed incredible, yet somehow typical
that the dynamic new cardiologist should learn in one
day a secret they had successfully kept from the whole
hospital for nearly a year.

'Good evening, Mr Trevalley,' Daniel Canaday said
evenly. His tone was quite different from the relaxed,
friendly one Rosalie had enjoyed over dinner. 'I left

some notes up here by mistake, Sister Crane. I came to get them. Did you happen to see them?'

'Um—I did see a black folder. . .'

'That's the one.'

'Well, I must be going,' Howard put in awkwardly. 'Sister Crane, thank you for your help with the—er—'

He didn't attempt to finish. He wasn't fooling Dr Canaday and all three of them knew it. He backed towards the still yawning lift, and its doors soon closed on his embarrassed figure, while Daniel's gaze continued to burn into Rosalie's with unmistakable disbelief, disappointment. . .and very strong desire.

She knew that her cheeks were on fire again, as they had been this afternoon, and when he spoke, in a low, intimate tone, she found that his question didn't come as a surprise. 'Are you really involved with *him*?'

It was her own answer, equally low-voiced, that shocked her. 'Not really. Not seriously.' They were standing very close to each other now. She knew that he must be aware of her quickened breathing, and she could feel the heat that came from him and see the mist of dampness where his throat and collarbone met. 'We're not committed to each other in any way.'

'Good!' said Daniel Canaday. 'Because I rather think I'd like to be involved with you myself.'

CHAPTER TWO

'THAT black folder of yours is on my desk, I think,' Rosalie said thinly. 'I really must get back to work, so if you could come in and pick it up yourself. . .'

'Of course.' Dr Canaday strode towards the entrance to the ward, his tone quite matter-of-fact now. She couldn't be angry with him, since she had betrayed quite clearly her own physical response to him, but she was profoundly disturbed by what had happened and it was not until he had taken the folder—surely he couldn't have left it behind deliberately!—and left the ward that she was able to collect herself and get her mind on the job. The rest of the shift passed in a daze, and it was fortunate that there were no problems among her twenty-seven patients and eight staff.

It was also fortunate that the twenty-minute drive back to her neat stone cottage in the village of Torbury Bay was a quiet one at eleven o'clock at night, because she spent the whole of the trip with her eyes, hands and feet carrying out the task of driving quite automatically while her brain whirled over the subject of Daniel Canaday.

Why did she find him so disturbing? It wasn't the first time a man had paid her such obvious attention, although it *was* the first time it had happened since she had begun seeing Howard Trevalley. Was that it? Did she feel that Dr Canaday had trespassed on her commitment to Howard?

No, she decided. What she had said to the cardiologist—although she should definitely *not* have said it!—was the truth. She couldn't feel that the senior surgeon's diffident, private courtship required her to feel bound to him exclusively. If he wanted that from her, he would have to make his intentions clearer and express them more openly and forcefully.

Did she intend to go out with Dr Canaday, then, if he asked her? It seemed very likely that he would, after his open avowal of interest. Was she repelled by how frank he had been? Again, no. She already sensed that he wasn't the kind of man to force himself on a woman. She didn't even think that his frankness came from arrogance. He had simply been very confident that she would respond to ——

Oh, lord! Her physical response to him must have been blatant, and she hadn't even realised it. She wouldn't go out with him! The idea suddenly seemed far too dangerous. What could a good-looking man in his early thirties want from a woman half a decade older, on the verge of menopause? She was crazy to even be thinking about what had happened today, and even crazier to be comparing him to Howard in any way.

Firmly she shut off the whirling thoughts, put her car in the garage, fed the cat, had a cup of tea and went to bed.

'The ambulance will be here at any minute,' Rosalie told Daniel Canaday the next morning. She had spoken to him over the phone already today, but now he had arrived on the ward and this was their first face-to-face exchange since last night's embarrassing episode near the lift.

'Good. I'll wait,' was his response. 'The room's ready for her?'

'Yes.'

They were both too concerned with what was going on this morning to be aware of personal matters. The cardiologist was already impatient for the ambulance. 'I hope the journey hasn't been too tiring for her. We're really racing against time here. Dr Bartlett in

London was *very* reluctant to switch her to our transplant programme.'

'I know.'

'And he may well be right. The timing of this is *terrible*!'

The patient who was uppermost in all their minds this morning was a girl of twelve, Jackie Billings. She had already been a patient at a large hospital in London for some time, and for the last few months had been on their transplant list awaiting a donor. Now, her heart was failing rapidly, and at this crucial time her mother, a divorcee, had remarried and moved to Plymouth.

'Not that I'm saying Mrs Billings shouldn't have got married,' Daniel mused, half to himself. 'Mrs *Rogerson*, I should say. The mothers of heart patients have a right to their own lives as well, but. . .'

'It was a tough decision for everyone,' said Rosalie.

'And of course Bartlett is sceptical of our programme because it's so new.'

'But we've done well in a year!' Rosalie protested, protective of the new development at her hospital. 'Our success-rate is as good as any in the world, and our transplant *people* aren't new. Mr Myers had three years in America working as a surgeon under Norman Shumway, not to mention your experience on the medical side in Cleveland.'

'And her chances of a donor match are the same here as in London,' Daniel came in.

Both of them were rambling a little, neither of them fully listening to the other, each more focused on the doors to the ward, waiting for them to open to bring in the new patient ensconced on a stretcher.

'I'll go down to the ambulance bay, I think,' Daniel said now.

'Don't,' Rosalie came in quickly. 'You might miss her in the lift.'

'You're right.'

And at that moment Jackie Billings arrived. 'Is Mum here?' was her first question, even before she reached the small private room that was waiting for her.

'No, she's not here,' Rosalie said, trying to act as if this were normal. She had assumed that Mrs Rogerson would be travelling down from London by plane and ambulance with Jackie, and now she held her breath, waiting for tears from the fragile-looking girl.

But no tears came. Jackie had a pixie-like little face, with big blue eyes and a button of a nose above a small, tidy mouth. 'I expect it's the twins,' she said matter-of-factly.

'The twins?' Daniel queried. He and Rosalie were walking beside their new patient to her room. No other medical staff had arrived yet. Peter Myers and his team were still in emergency surgery as they had been for half the night.

'Yes, my stepbrothers,' Jackie was saying. 'They're four years old and a bit of a handful. Mum's starting them at day-care today and she warned me she might be late. She's trying awfully hard not to be a wicked stepmother in their eyes, you see.' The little face showed an adult wisdom as she looked up at her new cardiologist, then she slumped tiredly back in the stretcher.

'Don't talk too much, love,' Rosalie said. 'Your mother will explain everything when she comes.'

'No, but she wouldn't explain about being scared of being a stepmother,' Jackie pointed out, and Rosalie caught Daniel's quick smile that said, This one's going to be interesting!

Moments later, Jackie was in her new bed, surveying the room with experienced eyes. Hospitals were far too familiar to her already.

'Everything all right?' Daniel asked her.

'There's no window.'

'Yes, there is. Over here.'

'That's not a window!' Her scorn for the narrow

panel of glass that, unfortunately, looked out onto a blank brick wall, was very apparent. 'There's no view, and anyway, I can't see it from where I am.'

'True,' said the cardiologist on a controlled sigh. The window was behind her left shoulder, requiring an impossible twist to see it from the bed. The most that could be said for it was that it brought some natural light into the room, and not much of that.

After some more casual chat, the cardiologist got down to business, going over the huge wad of notes and test results that had accompanied the new patient and asking a battery of questions. Rosalie stayed on hand to learn as much as she could, and it was some time before they came away. Mrs Rogerson had not yet arrived.

'My God!' breathed Daniel when they were safely out of Jackie's hearing.

'Yes. . .' agreed Rosalie. 'Her body might be tired out with that heart not able to do enough work, but her mind certainly isn't!'

'I'm thinking more of her resilience emotionally,' he said.

'You don't think it's a front?'

'No, I don't. She's more adult than many adults I've met.'

'That happens, sometimes, with serious childhood illness.'

'We owe this girl a lot, Sister Crane, she's putting up such a fight!'

'We owe her a new heart,' Rosalie retorted.

'And if we can't find that. . .'

There was a silence. They both knew that it was only a matter of weeks, and that Daniel's increasingly fine-tuned balancing act with a bewildering array of medicines and machines would, in the end, not be enough to keep the ailing heart alive.

The cardiologist went to see some other patients, forgetting to say goodbye to Rosalie, and she herself was distracted from conventional politeness by her thoughts of the new patient. She would have liked to stay with the girl until her mother arrived, but other duties called too strongly. Jackie was to be kept continually hooked up to an electrocardiograph machine at her bedside that was connected to a monitor here at the nurses' station, so that her heart rhythm could be seen at any time. A warning would bleep the moment there was any dangerous irregularity but still Rosalie found herself glancing at the monitor every minute. She also glanced at the door to the ward each time it opened, willing the new arrival to be Jackie's mother. Finally, half an hour later, it was.

She resembled her daughter very strongly, so Rosalie had no hesitation in going over and introducing herself. Mrs Rogerson was immediately in tears and would not go in to see her daughter until she had recovered.

'Jackie gets so angry when I cry,' she said. 'Can I wash my face?'

'Of course!'

'Is she all right? Did the journey tire her?'

'Well, yes, of course, but that was to be expected,' Rosalie pointed out, not yet sure how she felt about this woman. Did she really have Jackie's best interests at heart?

'We felt it was so important for her to be here in Plymouth, and so important for us to establish our new family properly now, in case. . .in case. . .there isn't a heart in time. It's what Jackie wanted — to know that things were settled and that she was here with us. I know Dr Bartlett was against it, but I think he's wrong.'

Rosalie nodded, her full sympathy aroused now. She could see Mrs Rogerson's point of view. If Jackie did lose her battle for life, she was the kind of person who would want to know that her family was settled and stable and would go on safely without her. 'In case

there isn't a heart,' Mrs Rogerson had said. That was
one of the hardest things about transplant surgery. For
Jackie Billings to live, someone else had to die at the
right time, someone whose body and blood types
matched Jackie's own. Rosalie had heard other transplant patients and their relatives express the guilt they
felt. 'Waiting for a heart. . .it's like wishing for someone else's child or husband to die.'

'No, not wishing for them to die,' Rosalie had said
more than once. 'They'd have died even if the word
"transplant" didn't exist. You're wishing for them to
have signed an organ donor card, or for their family to
feel that they can give life by donating kidneys and
corneas and heart. That's all.'

Mrs Rogerson went into the bathroom to wash her
reddened eyes and emerged, determinedly cheerful, a
few minutes later. Rosalie took her straight in to
Jackie, then left them alone together, and was able to
concentrate on her other patients now that she knew
Jackie was not alone. There was a message to say that
Mr Myers was on his way up here, as well.

It was not until after lunch that Daniel Canaday
appeared again. Rosalie encountered him as she
returned to the nurses' station after checking on a
post-operative transplant patient, a man of thirty-two
whose congestive heart failure had brought him within
a few weeks of death before a road accident victim's
heart became available. Now Richard Perry was doing
extremely well, and would soon be ready for discharge.
Seeing his young wife's face grow brighter every time
she visited her husband made the whole heart transplant programme worthwhile, in Rosalie's eyes.

'How is he?' Daniel asked immediately, guessing
that Rosalie had just come out of Richard Perry's
room.

'Better every minute, it seems.'

The casual response hid a mounting feeling of flut-
teriness inside her, and she realised that it had only

been their mutual concern over Jackie Billings this morning that had allowed her to repress her awareness of the new cardiologist. And if the glow in those black eyes of his was any indication, then he was feeling it too — not just a physical thing, but an emotional consciousness of some secret knowledge that they shared. It's that conversation over dinner about his father. I already feel I know him. . . But he can't have been serious about the two of us getting involved, she thought distractedly. He was just teasing because of seeing Howard and me. . . In fact, I should be angry with him. . .but I'm not! Damn! Everything she felt about him was ridiculous, inappropriate, dreadful!

To master these confused thoughts, she seized on the long tube of cardboard he was carrying and said, 'What have you got there? Some new gadget for our ward, fresh from America?'

'No!' he grinned, seeming as relieved as she was to find something safe to talk about. Somehow they were standing too close together. The package was almost brushing her shoulder, and she was aware of his warmth, and of the perceptive depth of those black eyes. She stepped a giddy pace backwards, thankful for sensible nurses' shoes. 'It's windows!' he said. She didn't understand him and he grinned again. 'For Jackie.' Then his voice dropped to a serious note. 'I'm crazy! I spent my entire lunch break in poster and art shops looking for these.'

He started to unfurl several large sheets of shiny paper from the cardboard tube. 'See! Pictures with windows in them. This is a Vermeer, or someone. This is some modern thing. I hope she appreciates it! Why did I do it?'

'I would have myself if I'd thought of it,' Rosalie consoled him, amused. Then she grew serious as well. 'You did it because you're worried about her and you had to do *something*.'

'So it makes sense to you? And you think she'll like them?'

'She'll love them. . .and I'm not worrying quite so much about her now because her mother has turned up and she's more responsible and concerned than we feared.'

'Good.' He touched her lightly on the arm and she took in a quick, startled breath that he did not miss. 'I'll take them in now, then.'

'I'll find some tape to stick them up with.'

'No need. I've got some newfangled poster putty that supposedly won't ruin the walls *or* the poster corners. Come and look in a few minutes when they're up.'

He strode off in the direction of Jackie's room and Rosalie returned to the nurses' station, thinking about the exchange. He found someting to do, she thought again. He was as worried about Jackie as I was and he couldn't stand it so he went out and *did* something. There was something very attractive in his direct response, she found.

And Jackie did love the posters. When Rosalie came in ten minutes later she was still imperiously directing the cardiologist from her bed. 'No, on second thoughts, that one should go on the far wall and this one on the side. This one I like the best so it goes where I can see it best, and too bad about a view for the visitors. They'll have to look at *me*!'

'So. . .like this?' Daniel said. It was the print of the Vermeer painting, with a serious, masterly quality to the composition that seemed to please Jackie's prematurely adult mind.

Rosalie stayed a moment then let herself out again quietly. Mrs Rogerson looked ten times more relaxed now, Daniel Canaday was clearly enjoying himself and would be careful to stop short of tiring Jackie too much.

'Now, if only there's a heart for her. . .' When it

came down to the crunch, that was all that really mattered.

'I'm afraid I'm going to have to cancel tonight,' Howard Trevalley said to Rosalie on Friday morning about ten days later. He leant confidentially and apologetically over her desk. 'It's short notice, I know.' It was just before half-past seven and he was about to leave for surgery after making an early round.

'I'm disappointed,' she said to him steadily, wondering if this was the truth.

'I know. But it can't be helped. My daughter has decided she wants to leave tonight, instead of tomorrow morning. Apparently there's some horse show she wants to see tomorrow, and it'll be half-over if we don't get to my sister's till lunchtime.'

'I quite understand, Howard, it's all right.'

She had known that he and his daughter were spending a weekend at his sister's place just beyond Exeter, and had been surprised that he wanted to stick to their habitual Friday night meeting. Howard himself seemed more irritated than she was by the change of plan.

'I thought Cathy would have outgrown this craze for horses by this time,' he grumbled. 'After all, she's twenty-six and a doctor. She should be taking serious steps to specialise by now, and instead she's talking about working in general practice for a few years before deciding what she wants to do. How can she expect to get to the top of any field—especially a *surgical* field—if she takes that lackadaisical attitude? There's no room for hobbies like horse-riding at her stage in a medical career!'

Rosalie made some soothing sounds. She had never met Cathy. So far, Howard Trevalley had kept his relationship with his ward sister a secret from family as well as from hospital staff. She had heard quite a bit about the young woman, however, much of it in this same vein. Reading between the lines, Rosalie had the impression that Cathy Trevalley must be a sensible, intelligent girl who enjoyed the family profession she had chosen. Clearly, however, she did not possess quite enough driving ambition to please her father.

'She might make a better specialist once she's experienced more of general medicine, though, mightn't she?' Rosalie ventured to suggest.

'Possibly,' Howard shrugged. 'Anyway. . .it spoils our Friday night.'

'Don't worry, I understand perfectly,' Rosalie assured him once again, and he stalked off to take the lift down to theatres, without saying goodbye.

Rosalie went to check on her patients and found several small matters that needed her attention. The swelling on Mrs Bunney's leg, where the saphenous vein had been removed to form a bypass vessel, wasn't going away quite as fast as it should. Mr Slade, spending his third day on this ward after quadruple bypass surgery and three days in Intensive Care, was still very disorientated and lethargic. Rosalie was starting to suspect a problem that hadn't been diagnosed.

And Mr Gupta wasn't coughing enough. He had been transferred here from Cardiac Intensive Care yesterday, and it was now four days since his triple bypass surgery. In many ways he was a good patient, quiet and uncomplaining, but his English was poor and Rosalie wasn't convinced that he understood the need to make himself cough in order to clear his lungs.

'Do some coughing for me, Mr Gupta,' she suggested once again, but was rewarded only by a weak sound, more like a polite 'Ahem!' than a cough.

'Come on, you can do better than that. Show him, Mr Rumbelow,' she said to an older man in the next bed who had been watching the exchange.

Mr Rumbelow obligingly broke into such an energetic cacophony of chest-clearing that Rosalie was afraid he would tire himself out for the rest of the day.

'Good, that's very good, thank you,' she said quickly, and he fell back on the pillows very proud of himself. Mr Gupta, however, was shaking his head fiercely and making pulling movements with his arm that looked like a mime artist pulling aside the lapels of an imaginary jacket.

Rosalie understood. Like all open-heart surgery patients, his chest had been split open for the operation and he was terrified that it would split again now as he coughed. 'Your chestbone is fine, Mr Gupta,' she told him. 'It's been put back together.'

He frowned, and made a mime of sewing.

'No, not with stitches,' she explained. 'With wires. Steel wires. Steel. Like this.' She banged the flat of her hand on the metal bed-rail. '*Ten* steel wires. It can't *possibly* come undone!'

She banged the bed once again for good measure then pressed her fists together and mimed an impossible struggle to pull them apart. At last it seemed to get through. Mr Gupta coughed again, tentatively at first. He frowned. It was painful.

'Yes,' Rosalie nodded. 'Of course it hurts, and you're on less medication now than in Intensive Care. Try again, and then have a rest. Let me pound your back a little, too.'

This time the coughs were what they should be, and Rosalie gave some rhythmic slaps to the man's bony back as well. He seemed to have the idea now, and his fear was lessened, but she had better remember to check on his coughing later in the day, and she would tell her juniors to remind him about coughing as well.

Speaking of juniors. . .'There's a patient being admitted,' Elise Jones said excitedly. 'An emergency. From Casualty.'

The girl was on her first extended stint of practical nursing. Pretty and blonde and lively, she flirted with all the male patients but was keen and bright at the

same time, and still alive to the frequent dramas of a
cardiac ward.

'Dr Canaday wants you to see him, and he'll be here
in a minute. I mean,' she added carefully, 'Dr Canaday
wants you to see the *patient* and Dr *Canaday* will be
here in a minute.'

She darted away again and Rosalie returned to the
nurses' station to receive the patient, while she mentally reviewed their spare beds. There were only three
of them, but as she didn't yet know anything about the
admission she couldn't decide which of the three it
should be. 'An emergency,' Elise had said, but if it
was truly one the patient would have been taken to
Cardiac Intensive Care.

The question was answered a few minutes later when
the patient, a fifty-three-year-old man who had suf-
fered what was tentatively diagnosed as a mild heart
attack, was brought in.

'Bed seventeen,' Rosalie decreed. The second bed
in one of the ward's several four-bed rooms, it would
be a reassuring place for someone in Mr Legge's
position, with two cheerful bypass patients who were
almost ready to go home, and one older man awaiting
a coronary angiogram, otherwise known as cardiac
catheterisation. This was the exploratory procedure
that Mr Legge would probably undergo himself within
the next few days.

He was soon ensconced in bed, and Rosalie sent
Margaret Binns to take routine observations, including
pulse, respiration and the body weight from which his
doses of medicine would be calculated. Margaret
would also give the new patient information about
ward routine and ask an extensive series of questions
about his medical history, covering everything from
allergies to appendicitis. Doctors needed to know such
details as whether he wore contact lenses or false
teeth, what his average alcohol consumption was. . .
the list went on and on. Finally, any questions that Mr

Legge had himself would be answered, although often those answers took the form of, 'We'll have to see what the doctor says.'

Dr Canaday appeared on the ward fifteen minutes later. Rosalie had been steeled nervously for his arrival, but she needn't have worried. He was obviously busy and simply tossed her a casual greeting, asked her the new patient's bed number and disappeared into the room. Rosalie returned to work, wondering how long this distracting situation could continue.

She was so aware of Daniel Canaday now, and she knew he was equally aware of her. She encountered him every day, and almost every time they met there was heat between them. She knew that he noticed if his arm accidentally brushed hers, and sometimes suspected feverishly that he made the contact deliberately. At ward or bedside conferences she felt his eyes on her and wondered that no one else seemed to have noticed the way they kept looking at each other — because her own gaze was drawn to him constantly, too.

That restlessness she had felt earlier last week seemed trifling compared to how she felt now, and she would swear that the cliff-top path was perceptibly deeper and more rutted now from the walks she took there almost every day to clear her head. . .

He was back from Mr Legge's bedside sooner than she expected, and when he stopped at the nurses' station and she realised that she was alone here, in a rare moment of calm on the ward, she knew that he didn't want to talk about the new patient's case history.

'I hear your usual escort has stood you up tonight. . .' he began in a low voice.

'Please. . .'

'Don't worry. I know the thing is a secret, and it's safe with me.'

'If you want——'

'What I want is to ask you out tonight.'

'Oh, I can't, I'm sorry, I——'

'You told me last week that Trevalley doesn't have exclusive dibs on your time. Dinner, that's all.'

'No, but I——'

'No?'

'No.' She looked up at him, rich colour suffusing her cheeks in dramatic contrast to her pale skin, vivid hair and chocolate-brown eyes. Their gaze locked and held. It was becoming a commonplace event but it still set Rosalie's heart pounding every time. She waited for him to argue her answer, but he didn't.

'In that case,' was his short response, 'I'll be going. I have a heavy schedule in the cath lab this morning.'

'All right, yes. We've got Mrs Stivens ready to send down to you now,' Rosalie answered, her tongue feeling like cotton wool.

'And I've altered Jackie Billings's medication a little after some discussion with Peter Myers. It's all noted down.'

He was gone a moment later, leaving her to wonder why she had said no. She found the answer to the question quite quickly. She was afraid of this, afraid of the strength of her response to him, and of his masterful frankness about his attraction to her.

The busy hours that followed came as a relief, and the successful emergency defibrillation of a pre-operative bypass patient in the middle of the afternoon brought a welcome sense of professional triumph. The moment when the electric current applied to the patient's chest jolted his heart into life and into a steady rhythm was always a supremely rewarding one. In spite of the fuss created by the emergency, she was able to leave promptly at three, and arrived home, after doing some errands, determined to tackle the garden properly for two or three hours—longer if the weather and light held up. She needed to occupy mind and body, and those trays of seedlings she had bought on the weekend badly needed planting.

But not all of them got planted that day after all. She had changed into her dark mulberry denim overalls, which smelled fresh from the laundry, teaming the comfortable garment with a bright pink cotton jersey beneath, and had been padding about her crooked stone paths in old white trainers for less than an hour when a low white car pulled up outside the front gate, and when she looked up to see if it was someone coming to the cottage she immediately recognised the energetic figure that sprang from the driver's seat.

'Hello,' said Daniel Canaday, his black eyes narrowing a little as he smiled at her. 'Thought I might find you out here. I got stubborn and came to see if you'd like a chance to reconsider tonight.'

'H-how did you know where I lived?' she gasped, feeling absurdly embarrassed at having been caught in her gardening clothes.

He stood on the far side of the picket gate and she approached him slowly, willing her breathing to return to normal.

'Some astute and very discreet probing of Howard Trevalley,' he answered her, 'followed by a chat with Mrs Batey at the corner shop here in the village.'

'I might have known it. Clever of you. . . But you shouldn't have come,' she finished very firmly, arriving at the gate and reaching down to undo the catch. Politeness demanded that she at least let him into the garden.

'Shouldn't I, Rosalie?' Suddenly, with the gate still between them, he was leaning over her and had taken her hands in his, imprisoning them in a caressing grasp. She felt his breath whisper in her hair as she stared down at their entwined fingers and heard him continue in an even lower tone, 'I couldn't get to the bottom of this on the ward this morning, but. . .should I really not have come?'

'Why *did* you come?' she gasped. The gentle pressure of his fingers massaging hers was electric.

'Isn't it obvious?' he said. 'Haven't I made it perfectly, painfully clear over the past ten days or so that I fancy you like mad and want to get to know you better? And don't you feel the same way?'

'Yes. . .no. How can you say this? We hardly know each other.'

'And how do you suggest we get to know each other if we don't spend any time together away from the hospital?'

'Please. . . Dr Canaday. . .'

'Daniel, for heaven's sake!' he exploded suddenly. 'My God, Rosalie, you're behaving like a Victorian miss. And yet I can't have. . . I *know* I haven't misinterpreted what you feel. How could I have? Look at you! You're not exactly pulling away from me!'

And it was true. With her hands still caught in his across the low gate, she was practically leaning against his shoulder for support as he bent towards her, her forehead almost brushing the strong clear jaw, and strands of her wayward mane of rich red hair mingling with the dark curls, slightly too long, that fell just behind his ears.

Physically, he exerted a magnetic pull over her that she had never experienced before. She was intensely conscious of his strong torso and long thighs, of the dent in the middle of his full upper lip, and the tiny white scar that edged his right jawline, of his wavy hair, his hard, muscled forearms, his columned throat and the clean male scent that hovered about him. But she mistrusted this physical response profoundly. It was too soon, too sudden, too dramatic. He could be a man who was accustomed to provoking this response in women, and who used it. . .

'Well?' he demanded, pulling her still closer so that

both their thighs pressed uncomfortably against the wooden pickets of the gate. 'You have to give me some kind of an answer.'

And she realised that in her turmoil she had been silent for far too long. 'Come inside,' she said abruptly. His hands were caressing her waist now. In a moment he would be kissing her and she longed for the touch of those dented lips with a wantonness that appalled her. 'We can't stand here with the whole world looking on.'

She pulled away and fumbled with the catch of the gate while he cocked an eyebrow at her last absurd statement. The cottage was at the end of a short lane and the house opposite was a weekender belonging to a couple from London. Down the road, Mr and Mrs McGonigal spent most of their time ensconced in front of the television. There was no one to see or care if they kissed over the gate for minutes on end. Leading the way inside, she regained a semblance of control, but this was soon unravelled when he rounded on her as soon as the front door was safely shut behind them.

'Now, Rosalie, please tell me why you're having a problem with this. You're not married, are you?'

'No. . .'

'And I assure you that I'm not, so there are no spouses to appear at a scandalously intimate moment brandishing jealous weaponry.'

'Actually, I'm a widow. . .'

There was an abrupt silence as he halted in the middle of the cream Berber carpet on which he had been pacing in evident frustration. 'Oh, Rosalie!' he whispered, shocked. 'I'm so sorry. That must have hurt. Lord, I'm a tactless idiot!'

'No,' she blurted desperately, coming to face him and touching his arm, unwilling to let this misunderstanding slip by, although it might have been a convenient one if it helped to put a safe distance between them. 'Not a recent one. It's not painful in that way any more. My husband died fifteen years ago.'

'Fifteen! You must have been a child when you married!' He searched her face as he spoke.

'I was eighteen,' she answered. 'I was twenty-two when he died. He was thirty-four. And now I'm thirty-seven.'

'Thirty-seven? Yes, I'd thought you must be about that. . .' Then he added suddenly, 'You don't mean to tell me it's the age-difference that's bothering you? That's absurd! *Completely* absurd!'

'No, it isn't.'

'It *is*! There was a. . .what?. . .twelve-year gap between you and your husband. You've just said so.'

'That's different. It's different when it's the other way around.'

'Why?' he demanded.

'Oh, must I go into it?' She broke away from him and began pacing the room as he had done moments before. She couldn't believe that this electric scene was taking place. They were arguing like old lovers, not like two people who had met for the first time less than two weeks ago. 'It's obvious! I was mature enough to marry at eighteen, and many girls are. I doubt that you would have been. Now I've lived half a life. I'm middle-aged, while you're only entering your prime, only just finished your years as a student. You're going to have twenty-year-old nurses throwing themselves at you every week, pretty blondes without the slightest hint of a wrinkle or a sag, while I'm past my best and it would be only charitable to label me "attractive".'

Rosalie spoke passionately, and she honestly thought that she was telling the truth. Thoroughly accustomed to her unusual colouring, she took it for granted and had no idea of the stunning impact it created, nor did she see, when she looked in the mirror morning and night, the vivid array of expressions that

crossed her face in the course of a busy day —
expressions that spoke of a rich emotional depth and a
warm concern for everything and everyone around
her. As for her figure. . . When she was confronted
daily by reed-thin models in every magazine, and
heard the younger nurses agonising over the slightest
bulge on hips, thighs or tummy, how could he value
the ripely curved maturity of her own shape?

'Charitable to call you attractive!' Daniel Canaday
exploded after a spluttering pause. 'When you rushed
into that meeting last week, with your cheeks like — '
He broke off, then continued urgently, 'Rosalie Crane,
you are just about the most beautiful creature I've
ever seen.'

'Really?' she answered spiritedly. 'Then, Dr
Canaday, you need to spend more time away from
your work!'

They looked at each other helplessly for a minute
and then to Rosalie's utter relief the tension vanished
in a burst of shared laughter. He flung himself down
on the pretty floral couch behind him, she let herself
relax into a matching armchair, and a comfortable
silence reigned for a minute or two as they caught their
breath.

'Did any of that resolve anything?' he asked gently
at last.

'I don't think so,' she responded equally gently, and
quite sincerely.

If anything, the fact that he so easily labelled her
'beautiful' only added evidence to the idea that he
wanted to consummate their physical attraction to each
other in a sizzling but short-lived affair. Strangely,
though she felt calmer, and for the first time it occurred
to her to wonder if a short, sizzling affair was exactly
what she needed. If that was all this was to be, then its
suddenness, its physicality and the age-difference
between them wouldn't matter.

'Is it really the age-difference?' he asked softly, as if

reading her mind. 'Or are you more seriously involved with Howard Trevalley than I thought?'

'No, I'm not,' she responded hesitantly. 'At least, he. . .we. . .it's a friendship at this stage, that's all.' Then, in an attempt to protect herself that she didn't fully understand, she added. 'But if it were to develop into anything more, then he has a lot to offer, and it would be a very suitable and sensible relationship.'

'Suitable and sensible,' he mimicked cruelly. 'If that's your attitude, then I can just imagine the evenings you two have together. You probably have a regular outing every second Thursday, and you go to dinner. I bet he takes you to Baldwin's!'

'How did you know?' she gasped.

'You mean he *does*?'

'Yes. I mean, mostly.'

He gave a shout of laughter. 'Baldwin's!'

'What's wrong with Baldwin's?'

'Nothing, nothing. And I'm behaving badly.' He was pacing the room again. 'I'm ridiculing Howard Tevalley and I don't mean to. He's a nice man and a brilliant surgeon, but the idea of him. . .and you. . . and Baldwin's.'

'I like Baldwin's,' she returned defiantly, and not quite truthfully.

'Rosalie, you've got ten times more life in you than you think! A hundred times more.' He came to her without warning, pulled her out of the armchair and on to her feet, and a second later his arms had snaked around her and he was holding her against him. 'Won't you let me prove it to you?'

'H-how?' The indignation she had felt a few moments ago was immediately swamped by such a surge of desire for him that it was difficult to speak.

'Nothing too frightening,' he murmured teasingly. He brushed his lips through her hair then trailed them lightly and tantalisingly across her forehead. 'I won't even kiss you,' he promised throatily. 'Not yet. Not properly. But how about dinner?'

'At Baldwin's?' she questioned slyly, drawing herself away from his touch with an effort.

'No! But I'll give you a choice. Take-away fish and chips on the beach, with a bottle of white wine and a bowl of coleslaw. We'll watch the sun set over the water and we'll take off our shoes and paddle.'

'Too cold,' she answered, thinking regretfully that the unusual picnic did sound rather carefree and nice. 'And they're forecasting rain.'

'Are they? Damn! Oh, well. . . In that case, it comes down to spaghetti carbonara at my place, or a little restaurant I know called Chez Guillaume, where you never know what's going to be on the blackboard menu from one day to the next.'

'Oh! Chez Guillaume! That sounds lovely,' she said quickly, too frightened by the prospect of an evening alone at his place.

He wasn't fooled by her apparent interest in the restaurant. 'Chicken!' he taunted lightly, and she knew that he had guessed exactly why she had rejected the suggestion of spaghetti carbonara.

But he seemed satisfied enough with her choice and she wondered what would happen if she called his bluff and said, On second thoughts, let's go to your place. Did he have the ingredients for spaghetti carbonara? Did he even know how to make it? *She* certainly didn't!

'Toss me that newspaper, then, and I'll read it while you go and change.' He was already clad quite suitably in dark trousers and a pale, silvery grey shirt.

'Oh, do you think I need to change?' she said sarcastically, smoothing the worn mulberry denim with her hands as if it were the latest couturier design from Paris. 'I thought we were being spontaneous.'

'Actually, I love the way those overalls hug the shape of your—— Never mind!' he broke off and grinned unrepentantly at her, apparently enjoying the blush that warmed her face as she guessed what he had been about to say.

'I'll change,' she said huskily, and fled up the carpeted stairs.

CHAPTER THREE

But what to change into, that was the question. There was really only one dress that seemed right, an ivory jersey silk that moulded her figure with soft, flattering lines. Too flattering, perhaps. She did not know if she could bear to have him devouring her with those dark eyes all evening, when all it made her want to do was respond to the open invitation in his face and fall into his arms. Had she ever been so aware of a man's body, and of her own?

Taking several deep breaths to steady herself, she pulled a very sedate cotton slip over her head, and then the dress, letting it fall in silky folds to just below her knees. The fabric seemed to caress her like soft fingers and even the very modest neckline, which revealed only the creamy skin of her throat and collarbone, seemed too daring.

Adding low-heeled ivory leather shoes and a slender gold locket and chain around her neck, she began to feel calmer. Clear lipgloss, a touch of mascara, no perfume—somehow that seemed too sensual—and finally a vigorous brushing of her hair so that it hung in a protective, bell-like halo of thick waves around her head and ended just below her shoulders.

'Ready,' she told him breathlessly as she descended the stairs.

He stood up and came to meet her, saying nothing. But if she had any doubts about his reaction to her appearance they were allayed when he helped her into a light spring coat of soft sapphire-blue. His fingers brushed the nape of her neck, his palms rested on her shoulders, and then he turned her into his arms and bent towards her, seeking her lips.

51

'No, please, n-not yet,' she gasped, the words betraying her knowledge that their kiss was inevitable. She was swollen with desire for him and it terrified her. She at least needed the comparative safety of dinner and conversation before she succumbed to the onslaught of their mutual physical need.

He didn't try to overcome her resistance, but released her slowly sighing with ragged-edged control at the same time. 'Hungry, are you?' he said lightly. 'So am I.'

The restaurant was quite a drive away, beyond Plymouth and across the Tamar. It was small and intimate, but there was no opportunity to eat at a secluded table out of sight of the other diners, as there was at Baldwin's. Daniel didn't seem to mind this in the least. He took no notice whatsoever of the other tables, almost all of which were filled.

'Will we get a place, do you think?' Rosalie asked.

'I booked over the phone while you were changing,' he answered. 'This is our table here, I should think.'

He was right and they were soon seated there, out of the way of the traffic of waiters and diners but quite close to several other tables. Thinking of the almost furtive way in which Howard always made sure there was no one from the hospital in sight, Rosalie felt a spurt of irritation against the older cardiac surgeon. Daniel Canaday's attitude was much more. . .invigorating. Why *did* Howard mind so much about the possibility of discovery? Was he ashamed of their friendship, or whatever it was? Any sense that she was betraying him by having dinner with Daniel tonight disappeared as she thought all this.

If Howard wants me, she decided to herself, he had better make it clear, do something about it. Would she marry Howard if he asked her? Six months ago, she realised now, she probably would have done. Now, she was far less sure. . .

* * *

'Now. . .he makes his own chocolates, too,' Daniel said. 'And they're unbelievable with coffee and liqueurs.'

'Oh, I *couldn't*!' Rosalie groaned.

'Yes, you could. You must!' he insisted. 'Don't you have a *tiny* corner in there? And *don't* tell me you're on a diet!'

'No, I'm not, but ——'

'Thank God for that! If there's one thing I loathe it's a dieting woman,' he said with feeling. 'In America they all are, it seems.'

'Really?'

'Even if they look like toothpicks already. And do they *talk* about it! "Are your hot-dogs ninety-eight per cent fat-free, or only ninety-two per cent fat-free?" "Will you have the low-cholesterol imitation blue cheese dressing on your salad, or the honey almond soy bean artificially sweetened creamy Ranch-style?"'

'Well, after that tirade, I'll have to have the chocolates, won't I, to save my reputation?'

'Wise decision.'

Their meal had been fabulous. Marinated goat's cheeses, tiny succulent prawns with a ginger dressing, medallions of pork in a rich, fruit-filled sauce. Berry soufflé for dessert. . .and now chocolates and coffee.

As she waited for these to arrive, Rosalie said thoughtfully, 'Daniel, you're a cardiologist. I'd have thought you'd be in favour of these new low-fat things, and people's increased awareness of the dangers of cholesterol.'

'What I'm in favour of is a genuine change in lifestyle,' he answered energetically. 'And I'm often afraid that this "ninety-eight per cent fat-free" business is going to fool people into thinking they're health-conscious when in fact "ninety-eight per cent" of their bad habits remain unchanged.'

'Hmm. . . Give me an example.'

'This is shop-talk. Are you sure you want to?'

'Yes. I like to hear the latest health news from across the Atlantic. And since you've recently returned from the Cleveland Clinic. . .'

And, in fact, it was the first time the talk had turned to professional matters all evening. Rosalie wondered in a slightly bewildered way how they had managed to occupy over two hours without turning to the most obvious thing they had in common, but she didn't have time to give the question much thought. She was too interested in what he was saying about hamburgers.

'Some of the big fast-food chains have new fat-free hamburgers out. I dare say they have arrived here by now, but I'm not a fast-food fan so I wouldn't know. But what they're finding in America, apparently, is that a large percentage of the people who used to have a plain old fatty hamburger are now having a nice, new fat-free hamburger with double cheese. . .'

'Thus consuming just as much fat and cholesterol as before, while under the impression that they're doing something for their health. I begin to see your point,' she said.

'People are switching to six cans of diet soft drink a day, instead of the sugar-sweetened kind, and considering it a great victory for health. I don't want to see someone eating a hunk of fat-free chocolate cake topped with artificially sweetened dairy-whip, I want to see them eating a fresh fruit salad.'

'Not exactly the sort of healthy fare we've eaten tonight,' she reminded him.

'I know. I eat healthily most of the time but when I do splurge on rich food I make it the genuine article. Real egg-filled cakes, decent cheese, pure chocolate. Don't you agree?'

'Yes, I do, but you're making me review my own day-to-day eating habits. Do they really compensate for a splurge like this?'

'I'm sure they do.'

'How do you know?'

'I've seen that vegetable garden of yours. All those lettuces and carrots and herbs coming on so nicely in the spring sunshine.'

'All right, then. I won't feel guilty about that soufflé.'

'Don't. I mean, have you ever tasted fat-free cake?'

'No. Have you?'

'Purely in the interests of medical research, I hasten to say. It's like eating old foam rubber.' He paused and then they added in unison, 'Artificially flavoured foam rubber.'

Then she said a little hesitantly, 'I have another question, too. Do you mind if we talk shop for a bit longer?'

'Not at all, if you don't,' he said, raising one eyebrow. 'I'm a highly qualified specialist, remember? We love what we do.'

'Well, then. . .the transplant programme. You so often seem to be on the side of medical rather than surgical treatment of heart problems, yet you're so involved in the transplant programme. Isn't that a contradiction?'

'Not for me,' he answered her seriously. She thought in passing that the planes of his face fell very attractively when he was serious, too. 'My aim is to find and use the most appropriate kind of care and treatment. With some people, lifestyle change is the key. But with others, when there's no hope that a heart can keep going. . .'

'Like Jackie. . .'

'Like Jackie,' he agreed, 'then transplant has to be the answer.'

'Yet so many people, particularly among the general public, still think heart transplants are straight out of Dr Frankenstein's lab.'

'That's unfortunate,' he nodded, frowning. 'But it has been like that with every major medical advance in history. Immunisation, even anaesthesia. . . Expensive, radical treatments like heart transplants can't be the only direction in which medicine is pushing forward, but there's a place for it. What's really a pity is that some of the early specialists in the field were more concerned with becoming celebrities than with perfecting the procedure. It got a bad name as a result. But now, with the new improvements in drugs that suppress the body's rejection mechanisms, and with all the patient, detailed work that people like Norman Shumway have done over the years. . .'

Rosalie listened, nodded, made an occasional comment. It all made a lot of sense, and it was the first time since the transplant programme had started at St Bede's that she had been able to thrash out the issues like this. Theoretically they were discussed at the regular fortnightly transplant programme meetings that she always attended, but these meetings were only an hour long and there was always so much else of a more practical nature to talk about, and so many other voices to be heard.

As well, Daniel talked to her as an equal, as interested in her comments as if she had been a specialist at his own level. 'My brain feels thoroughly exercised now!' she laughed, after quite an argument about the ethics of matching organ donor and recipient.

'Does it feel good?' he teased lazily.

'Yes!'

They lingered for another half an hour over the coffee and chocolates, and Rosalie still didn't want to leave. There was some magic about this evening and this restaurant, and she didn't want to break it by going out into the open air. For two and a half hours she had been able to put aside much of her disturbing awareness of this man, had stopped comparing him with Howard and with Mike, hadn't been wondering and fretting about the physical pull between them and what it meant, what he wanted from her.

Instead, she had been getting to know him as a person, and there was no doubt that she liked what she was beginning to find. His energy stimulated her, the decided nature of his opinions made for zesty discussion, and the strong suspicion she had gleaned already at the hospital that beneath his dynamic exterior lay a thoughtful and sensitive soul was being rapidly confirmed.

She could have stayed here a lot longer, but it really was time to leave. The drive home didn't seem as long as the drive in the other direction, and they were both rather silent. With a mixture of relief and disappointment, Rosalie decided that perhaps she would not end the evening in his arms after all, and when he pulled up outside her gate and switched off the engine she said sincerely, 'That was a marvellous evening, Daniel. I enjoyed every minute of it.'

'I'm glad you did, and so did I, but. . .'

Rosalie went on quickly, 'There's no need to see me inside,' and she had her hand on the door as she spoke.

'Hey! Hang on! Of course I'll see you inside.' He sprang out and was beside her door, opening it for her, before she could work the handle from her own side. 'I'm not going to kiss you in the car,' he added in a caressing whisper as he reached a warm hand down to pull her to her feet.

There! All he had to do was mention the word and she was melting. She couldn't find an answer to his words so there was only the crunch of shoes on stone as they walked up the front path together. Was she really going to allow him inside the house when it was after eleven at night, though? She stopped in the small, sheltered porch and turned to him, although she didn't yet know what she was going to say.

In the end, however, he was the one to speak. 'I don't think I can wait until we get inside,' he murmured, and then she was in his arms and his firm mouth was tasting her lips hungrily.

She made no effort to hold back her own response.
Had she tried to, she suspected she would have found
it impossible. He held her closely at first so that their
bodies were pressed together from shoulders to thighs,
then as the demand of his lips increased he released
her a little so that he could run hot fingers over her
gently rounded hips and trail them upwards till they
cupped the fullness of her breasts through the thin,
figure-hugging jersey.

Rosalie's own fingers splayed against his hard chest,
and she felt the urgent rise and fall of his breathing
that matched her own. Then, for a moment, he
released her mouth to whisper raggedly, 'I want you
so badly, Rosalie!' and her lips framed a response
seemingly by themselves.

'I know. I want you too.'

She had never before expressed her desire to a man
so frankly and nakedly. Even with Mike, more than
three years into their marriage, she had been very
reticent and had rarely succeeded in matching his level
of arousal and fulfilment. The words she had just
spoken seemed to echo around them, although she
had barely voiced them aloud, and suddenly all her
fears came flooding back. How could she trust something this passionate, this abandoned?

He pulled away from her seconds later. 'I'd better
go,' he said, 'before. . . Well, it's late. I want to be in
at the hospital first thing tomorrow. And I'm on call,
starting at midnight, until seven on Monday morning.'

'I have an early shift, too,' she managed.

'That settles it, then.'

'Yes.'

'I'm sure I'll see you on the ward.'

'It's where I'll be.'

He bent towards her and brushed her small nose
lightly with his own very strong and masculine one.
'Can't wait, actually. . .' Then he blurred into the
darkness down the path and for a moment she thought

he wasn't going to say anything more, but was simply about to jump in his car and drive away. At the gate, though, he turned and called back.

'Got your keys?'

'Yes. . .' She had just closed fumbling fingers over them in her white beaded evening bag.

'Good. I'll wait until I see a light on upstairs before I drive off, all right?'

'Thanks.'

And, alone in her room three minutes later, she heard the engine hum into life and then die away as his car wound back through the village. She listened to the sound shamelessly until she couldn't hear it any more.

'Did you have a hot date last night, Sister Crane?' Elise asked daringly the next morning during the routine nurses' conference that took place at the change of shift. Rosalie had yawned three times already, but none of the other juniors would have dared to refer to the fact in such a suggestive way, although two of them giggled at Elise's words.

'I didn't sleep very well, that's all,' the ward sister answered, half truthfully, wondering whether she should have frowned down the question.

She didn't want to have to command respect by seeming rigid and humourless, but. . .was Elise going too far? She decided in favour of the girl after a moment's thought. There was deference behind the teasing, and Elise was always obedient and hard-working when it came to the real job of nursing.

'Mr Slade is definitely deteriorating,' the night sister, Louise Porter, reported with a frown as the group of nurses concentrated on their work once again. 'I think it's more than just post-operative disorientation.'

'I'll ask Dr Canaday to look at him as soon as he gets here,' Rosalie said.

'Oh, is he coming in this morning?' Margaret Binns asked.

'Um — yes, I think so,' Rosalie answered awkwardly, furious with herself.

She couldn't afford to blush and fumble with words like this every time the subject of Daniel Canaday came up. She was behaving like one of her own shyest student nurses with a painful crush! All in all, it was a relief when the ward conference was over, and the night staff had only just left when a slightly bleary-looking Dr Canaday arrived on the ward.

'You were called in?' Rosalie said sympathetically after one look at him.

'Yes, at two, and I was just getting ready to go back home when someone else was brought in. Is there any coffee going?'

'I'll get you some. And a biscuit as well.'

'Love one. Three, actually.'

'Three. . .'

'Three packets.' It was said very seriously, but she rewarded him with a laugh. 'Meanwhile,' he went on, 'I'll take a general tour. But is there anything specific to report from the night staff?'

'Yes, Sister Porter is concerned about Mr Slade. He's showing further signs of deterioration. Everyone else had a good night, though Mr Coggins was upset earlier.'

'I'll have a chat to him too, then. Mr Slade first, though.'

'Would you like me to be there?'

'Bring me the coffee first!'

To an incurious observer, it could have been an exchange between any doctor and nurse that were on casually friendly terms, but a closer look at the pair would have revealed what Rosalie was intensely conscious of — a dozen nuances of tone and gesture that spoke of their mutual awareness of each other, and of what had happened last night.

The coffee was soon made and, remembering how he had taken it strong and black last night, with no sugar, she didn't dilute the brew with boiling water as she usually did for herself. At Mr Slade's bedside, however, Daniel was too busy to think of the coffee after all. He was frowning, she saw, as he took the patient's blood-pressure.

'Take a deep breath, Mr Slade,' he said.

'Hmm?' the old man queried weakly.

'A *deep breath*.'

Labouring, Mr Slade did so, and Dr Canaday observed the level of the mercury in the sphygmomanometer carefully. Then he turned to Rosalie and held out a stethoscope for her. 'You might like to listen to this,' he said in a low voice that would not carry to his patient.

Rosalie did so, adjusting the instrument carefully in her ears. She heard a sandpapery sort of sound and looked at the cardiologist questioningly as she returned the stethoscope to him, after giving Mr Slade a reassuring pat on the shoulder.

'Friction rub,' he said. 'And his systolic blood-pressure goes down by fifteen points when he takes a deep breath.'

'You mean. . .?'

'Yes,' he said tiredly, 'I think it's fairly severe pericarditis. Not just inflammation, but infection and fluid as well.'

'Oh, no!' Rosalie murmured.

'I'm afraid so. I'll put him on the ECG and if that shows pericardial effusion and cardiac tamponade we'll have to do a pericardial window.'

Rosalie, familiar with the minefield of technical terms he had used, knew that this meant opening Mr Slade's chest again, opening up the pericardium — the covering around his heart — and cleaning and draining it of the fluid that was putting stress on his heart and creating abnormal heart rhythms.

'Then back to Intensive Care?' she suggested.

'Yes.'

They both knew that his chances of recovery now were weakened a little, but at least the problem had been pin-pointed. Pericarditis was a complication that occurred in mild form in about ten per cent of bypass patients, but Mr Slade's case seemed more severe, and he had gone into surgery as a high-risk patient to begin with.

'If he gets back here, you'll have him for quite a while,' was Dr Canaday's prediction. 'Now, we'll probably want to schedule surgery as soon as possible. . . Mr Forster is on call for surgery today, isn't he?'

'Yes. Do you want him paged now?'

'I'd like to call Max Hillston, get him to look at the ECG with me and hear what he has to say about the whole thing first. It's questionable whether Mr Slade will survive another opening up.'

They were walking back to the nurses' station as they talked, and Dr Canaday, with coffee in hand, narrowly escaped colliding with the darting form of Elise Jones as she hurried out of one of the four-bed rooms with a chart in her hand and a frown on her face. The student nurse gasped as she came chest to chest with the dynamic cardiologist, and he put out a hand with a lightning reflex to steady her.

'Oh, sorry, Doctor. . . Thank you,' she breathed.

'Don't want you slipping on these polished floors,' he said, then turned back to Rosalie. 'I have to go over to Outpatients for a minute, but I should be back by the time Dr Hillston's ready for me.' He strode ahead and had disappeared through the ward doors seconds later.

'Ohh!' Elise moaned, sagging dramatically against the wall with the back of her hand pressed across her brow. 'That man, Sister, that man!'

'What about him, Elise?' Rosalie said, her tongue feeling like cotton wool.

'Well, I mean, he's just outrageously gorgeous, isn't he?'

'Is he? I suppose so. He seems to be an excellent cardiologist, anyway.' The stiff tone and the prim reminder about Dr Canaday's more important role on the ward made Rosalie sound, to her own ears, about a hundred years old.

To Elise's ears as well, evidently. 'An excellent cardiologist?' she echoed vaguely. 'Oh, yes, of course he is. I'm sure he is. They all are, aren't they? But it's his looks that I'm pining over. Still, I suppose you wouldn't notice that sort of thing. . .in your position, I mean.'

She smiled sheepishly, and if she had been thinking, And at your age, she certainly didn't say it.

'No, I don't generally notice such things,' Rosalie forced herself to say, then she added with a firm note of admonition, 'What I *do* notice, though, is when my nurses are distracted from their work by silly crushes.'

'Oh, I know.' Elise blushed prettily. 'I'm not serious. He's probably in love with some gorgeous creature with a high honours degree in Ancient Greek and Old Norse who's about *twenty-five*!' She relegated the quarter-century mark to the vintage of middle-age with her tone.

'Why Ancient Greek?' Rosalie couldn't help asking.

'Oh, you know. Not Ancient Greek, necessarily, but *something*. She probably wears her hair in a bun and has big glasses with enormous frames, but when she takes them off and takes out those hairpins, wow!'

'And is she blonde, dark or redheaded?'

'Blonde, of course. No one ever believes blondes have any brains. I certainly don't have them! But he's discerning enough to have landed the one in a thousand who does.'

'You certainly have a vivid imagination, Elise!'

'I do, don't I? Still, it's very useful. Stops me from

making a fool of myself over men like Dr Canaday. But, Sister, I've got a problem with this chart. . .'

Suddenly, before Rosalie had time to catch her breath, the pert blonde student nurse was presenting her with a long query about the observations she had just done on Mrs Travis. It had been a somewhat unsettling exchange. . .

It turned out that Mr Slade did indeed have a major infection of the pericardium, and he had to be prepared for emergency surgery immediately after Max Hillston and Daniel Canaday had conferred together and confirmed the diagnosis through an ECG. Later that morning there was another emergency to be prepped for, too, a triple bypass on a man who had stubbornly resisted all attempts to treat his condition through medication and diet, and the two set-backs in their patients cast a rather gloomy atmosphere over the staff on the ward.

Rosalie tried to infuse some cheerfulness and energy, but found the task a little beyond her today. Elise's frivolously created brainy blonde haunted her, although she knew it was foolish, and memories of last night, his kiss and her deep awareness of Daniel Canaday, swept over her without warning at the most inopportune times, making her feel weak and out of control.

Strangely, once she got home, though, she didn't feel the weariness that she thought would overtake her after her bad night and long day. Instead, there was an aura of zest and energy about her and she put on a jazz record and half danced to it in the kitchen as she made a carrot cake then some macaroni cheese for her evening meal, as well as a crisp salad and wholemeal savoury loaf to freeze for future use.

Accomplishing all this in what seemed like a surprisingly short time, she got out her sewing patterns and a length of stiff rust-brown silk taffeta that had been sitting in her craft cupboard for months now. It really was time for a glamorous new dress. . .

And then the phone rang. 'Hi. . .' He didn't bother to say his name but she knew at once who it was.

'Hi.' A breathless response that gave away far too much about how she felt just at the sound of his voice.

'What are you doing?'

'Oh. . .sewing. Choosing a pattern, actually.'

'Sewing? On a Saturday night?'

'I've been at work all day, remember.' Anticipating his objection — that on a Saturday night she should be out on the town — she tried to speak severely, but failed. 'I'm too tired to go out.'

'But not too tired to sew.'

'I don't have to dress up to sit at home and sew.'

'You don't have to dress up to come out to coffee and a movie with me.'

'Well, if you could see what I was wearing. . .'

'I'd love to.'

'No, you wouldn't.'

'Describe it.'

'But anyway, I can't. . . I mean, isn't it too late for a film, especially with coffee beforehand?'

'No, not at all. It's half-past eight. I can be at your place by nine. There's a café next to the cinema and the late show starts at ten-fifteen. What time is your shift tomorrow?'

'Three till eleven.'

'So you'll be able to sleep in.'

'But you're on call.'

'I'll risk it. And you haven't told me what you're wearing yet.'

'Well, a very baggy purple jersey and jeans, so you see. . .'

'It sounds perfect.'

'Hang on —'

'I'll be there within half an hour.'

He had hung up — deliberately, she suspected —

before she had any further chance to protest his
suggestion, and there was a crazy part of her that
wanted to sing about it. The thought that she would
see him again in such a short time made her absurdly,
frighteningly happy. But she didn't take him seriously
about the purple jersey and jeans. Instead, after
distractedly and untidily packing away her patterns
and material, she pulled on the black wool skirt and
lacy cream blouse that she had worn several times
when she was with Howard. The outfit was neat and
smart, if not very adventurous, but it should be suitable for a casual evening at the cinema.

It was not. Or Daniel Canaday didn't think so,
anyway. He made that quite clear as his gaze swept
over her after she opened the door to him at three
minutes to nine. 'Hey! Where's the purple pullover?'

'You weren't serious, were you?' she answered,
taken aback. 'I couldn't have worn that. Not *out*.'

'Yes, you could! I was looking forward to seeing
that glorious contrast. Vivid purple, against this.' He
reached his fingers up to her hair, took a handful of
the glossy red fall of it and let it drop to her shoulder
again, the simple touch enough to inflame her beyond
the discomfiture she felt at his less than enthusiastic
response to her clothes.

'D-don't you like what I'm wearing?' she had to ask,
blurting the words and wishing them unsaid before
they were fully out of her mouth. What else could he
do but make some polite, complimentary protest?

He didn't, though.

'No, I don't,' he answered, typically direct. 'You
shouldn't wear black and white together.'

'It's cream.'

'Cream, then. Cream by itself is fine. Even black by
itself. . .' Then he noticed her frozen face, and suddenly she was in his arms and his mouth was whispering against her cheek and hair and ear. 'It's just that I
love your hair so much. . .and your eyes. . .and your

skin. I can't bear to see them drowned out by that prim colour scheme of yours. I want to see you in green or purple or rust. . .or in that goldy cream you wore last night that lets your hair flame as if it's really on fire. . .'

Sighing against him, she surrendered to the kiss that followed hard upon his words. The touch of his lips soothed away the bluntness of his earlier criticism and his sensuous praise of her hair melted her already thin defences against him. Soon, they were pressed together, with the soft fullness of her breasts crushed tenderly against his chest and the lean length of his thighs shored against her own legs like the trunks of two strong young trees.

She forgot that they were standing in the front hall, that they were supposed to be going to a film, that Cedric the cat would probably slip past her ankles and into the house, rebelling against his evening banishment. All that mattered was that Daniel's kiss was as wonderful as it had been last night, and that she was melting and tingling in nerve-endings she hadn't known she possessed.

'I'm sorry I was so blunt,' he said against her mouth after some time.

'It doesn't matter,' she murmured absently.

'Yes, it does. It's one of my principal faults.'

'No. I like it.' And her mouth melted against his once more.

'It's hell trying to stop this,' he groaned at last, and she felt the most turbulent desire to answer, then let's not. Let's not stop.

After all, she had been married for four years. She knew what greater heights of feeling could be attained in the abandonment of a bed. . .although even as she thought this there came the pulsing realisation that those heights with Daniel would be more fulfilling than anything she had experienced with Mike so long ago.

Reason prevailed, however, and as the cool evening

air came between them and both attempted to calm their quickened breathing she was relieved that she hadn't given in to that wild urge to go further with a man she still knew so little about. Dropping her spring coat around her shoulders, she locked the house and they went to his car together without speaking.

'Where is the cinema?' she asked when she could trust her voice again.

'Just a mile from the hospital. It's new. Very arty. Late shows every night. But I think we'll like this film. It's French. Can't remember the title. *Le* something.'

'Oh, I think I've heard of it,' she returned with deceptive mildness. 'No, hang on. That was *La* something.'

'Whatever it is, it's certain to have Gerard Depardieu in it. He seems to be in everything these days.'

The café was dimly lit and artily decorated, with opera playing quietly and a long menu of exotic coffees and cakes. If there was anyone at the tiny round tables *not* dressed in black, it was only because they wore magenta or crimson or orange instead, in the form of bright, skin-tight leggings or baggy pullovers or figure-hugging minis. Following Daniel to a table near the plant-filled windows, Rosalie overheard some alarming snatches of conversation.

'The dynamic of self-exposure in Mapplethorpe's work is. . .'

'Tiny, tiny slices of white Japanese radish. . .'

'I told Jason that if he was still involved with Linda *and* Rachel, then I'd go on seeing Brendan *and* John. . .'

She wondered if she really fitted in to this atmosphere of trendy debate and experimental relationships. Daniel pulled a chair out for her, taking not the slightest notice of any of these alarmingly Bohemian creatures, and Rosalie was glad of it. He had been right earlier. The purple pullover and jeans, with some

chunky jewellery and those soft grey suede boots she
hadn't worn in a long time would have fitted in here,
and she had the horrible conviction now that those
effusive words of his about colour were just tact on his
part.

What *did* he want from this, though? And, more
importantly, what did she. . .?

CHAPTER FOUR

'BUT it was only the shoddiest of souvenir issues, so I didn't buy it. He was quite disappointed, but I was adamant. The man knew nothing about numismatics at all!'

Howard Trevalley was talking about coins. Coin-collecting was his chief hobby, and, other than surgery and brief excursions into current affairs and the arts, his major topic of conversation. Rosalie sometimes found the subject quite interesting, as she had a soft spot for collectors. Her father, who had been almost fifty when she, his only child, was born, had collected stamps and had spent a lot of time talking to her about them years ago. Howard Trevalley didn't quite have the same story-teller's skill, though.

In fact, she was finding Howard very irritating tonight. Perhaps it was because he hadn't noticed her new dress. During a conspiratorial exchange at the beginning of the week, he had invited her to this restaurant. Not Baldwin's, but Idiosyncrasy, a very expensive and fashionable place in the centre of Plymouth, with impeccably starched crimson napkins and impeccably starched pale waiters. On a frivolous whim, she had decided immediately that she would get to work on that length of rusty red-brown taffeta and would have it finished by tonight.

By thoroughly neglecting her garden and working from before breakfast until late at night on her two days off, she had succeeded in her goal and she was very pleased with the result. The pattern she had chosen was a daring and dramatic one, included in a packet that contained two more conservative patterns for day-dresses which she had made last autumn.

When the dress was completed late last night she had tried it on before the full-length mirror in her bedroom and had felt a moment of misgiving at the way the stiff, ruched fabric hugged her waist and hips, and the low, gracefully shaped neckline revealed more than a hint of the pale, swelling mounds of her breasts and the deep cleft between them. Her last thought before going to bed had been that perhaps she wouldn't wear the dress for Howard after all, but today she had felt rebellious again. Compared with some of the wilder fashions made popular by pop stars on their music videos these days, a small *décolléte* was nothing to be shocked about.

And surely the dress would have to make Howard sit up and take notice. . .take notice of her as a woman . . .so that he made his intentions clearer, did something masterful and dramatic, swept her up into something passionate so that she didn't keep comparing him with Daniel Canaday, who always, in such comparisons, came out dangerously far ahead.

Daniel Canaday. Refusing to acknowledge to herself that the new cardiologist might be the real problem, she dismissed him from her mind — or tried to — and concentrated on the fact that she was angry with Howard about not noticing her dress. For heaven's sake! Anyone would think she had met him at the door in Saturday's black skirt and cream blouse which she now disliked heartily, instead of standing there posed — yes, she had to admit she had posed rather deliberately — and expectant, waiting for his praise.

Or at least *something*! Anything other than the blandly polite, distantly tender greeting Howard had given her. 'Good evening, my dear. How are you? Not too tired for this evening, I hope?' followed by a courteous and very brief touch on her back — with no caressing of the sensuous fabric — as he guided her down the front path.

She realised now as they sat here enjoying brandied

fruits for dessert that she was still waiting for a
compliment about her appearance. She knew that the
rust-coloured taffeta was shimmering with different
tones in the soft golden light of the restaurant, and
that the matt white of her skin above that controversial
neckline was as smooth as ivory, but he was frowning
across at her as if she were some fellow surgeon at a
tiring medical conference.

'You seem a little preoccupied tonight,' he was
saying to her, she found, and she started rather guiltily.
Had he still been talking about coins? She realised
with shame that she didn't know.

'Oh, yes. . . I am getting tired,' she answered, and
a yawn covered by her neat hand confirmed this. He
wasn't to know, thankfully, that the yawn was more
one of boredom.

'Yes, we should be getting you home,' he frowned.
'Perhaps you'd rather not have coffee this evening.'

'I think not, if you don't mind.'

'Not at all. Not at all.' But now it was his turn to
seem preoccupied, and she watched and waited, realising that he was searching for words. 'The weekend
with Cathy at my sister's went off well,' he said finally.

'Oh, good.' It wasn't what she was expecting.

'I told her a little about you, actually.'

'Did you?'

'Yes. I hadn't mentioned you before, but that began
to seem rather unnatural. After all, we're just friends,
at this stage. *Good* friends, I hope?' he added with
ponderous archness in his tone.

'Oh, yes. . .' she murmured automatically.

'But, yes, it seemed to me that there was no reason
not to mention you to my daughter, and so I did.'

'Oh, good.'

She didn't know what he expected her to say. Was
this a move forward in his eyes? If so, why on earth
couldn't he be more specific, more forthright? If it had
been shyness, she might have had more patience with

these slow, heavy-handed skirmishings, but she knew that he wasn't a shy man in any of his other dealings. Still, remembering that he had lost his wife two years ago, she felt her impatience and irritation subside.

'I had been wondering, though,' he went on now, 'if my idea earlier that we should go away together for a weekend was inappropriate. I'm afraid I embarrassed you. . .'

'Well, no, you didn't,' she assured him gently.

'Oh. Very well. But the fact remains, if anyone found out about it, it would be a bit sticky, wouldn't it? You know what people are like. . .'

'Yes,' she said on a controlled sigh, not prepared to challenge him.

Admittedly, a relationship between two people who worked together could create problems with other co-workers or even with the administration, but there was nothing illicit about this, no professional ethics had been violated, especially since he kept insisting that it was just a friendship. . .and it was, too, apart from those chaste, careful kisses.

Suddenly, Daniel Canaday filled her thoughts again. He had no qualms about what anyone might think, no qualms about hiding his desire for her in any way. They had almost been caught the other day, kissing in the lift, and by Elise Jones of all people. That was on Monday, two days after that evening at the cinema when his arm had slid around her moments after the cinema darkened so that she had spent the whole film bathed in a white heat of awareness and desire.

They had kissed in the car afterwards, kissed on her doorstep, and she had almost asked him to come in, but mutually, wordlessly, they had decided to pull apart before control and reason flew to the four winds, and that kiss in the lift had been a delayed, frustrated consummation that had made her resolve to be frosty towards him in sheer self-defence for the rest of the week.

She had kept her resolve, too, but she knew Daniel wasn't fooled into thinking she had suddenly changed her feelings towards him. She had agreed to go to an evening of classical ballet with him next week, and at the hospital the connection between them, even when they sat on opposite sides of the room at a ward conference, remained electric. This seemed to amuse the cardiologist. At any rate, there was a twinkle in his eye whenever their gaze locked, which seemed to be constant. What did the twinkle mean? What did he want from her? Sex? She was already achingly close to giving it to him and he probably knew it.

So there! Perhaps she should be gratified that Howard was so slow in moving forward. At least she could never claim that she had been rushed into something without having a chance to think. And perhaps caution was a good ingredient in the recipe for marriage, especially as one grew older and more set in one's ways. . .

'Yes, perhaps it *is* a bit soon to be talking about a weekend away,' she said to Howard now. 'After all, there's no rush for us to. . .to. . .'

To her relief he came in on top of her trailing words. 'No! Exactly! No rush at all!'

Half an hour later she had been courteously delivered to her door with only the smallest touch of his cool lips against her cheek.

Rosalie shifted in her seat. The orchestra was tuning up in its pit and the large auditorium of the theatre was alive with noise and colour as people greeted each other in the aisles and took their seats. The place was nearly full now. In a few moments, the overture to *Giselle* would begin and beside her Daniel's seat was still empty. She wasn't alarmed, knowing that he could be kept at the hospital by any number of emergencies or crises.

She did feel out of touch, though. Her shift yesterday had ended at three, and today she had had the day off. Coming into town by bus to do some shopping, she had taken longer than expected and had decided not to return home. Her dress would do very well. It was royal purple, so rich that it was almost indigo, and it was made of a clinging cotton jersey that hugged her figure with a simple, round-necked bodice before falling into a full calf-length skirt from the gathered waist. If she had a quick meal somewhere and freshened her make-up, she would be ready for the evening and Daniel could drive her home afterwards. He had said that he would if she needed him to, although he had been unable to pick her up at home.

'I'm coming straight from the hospital,' he had said. 'But I should be there by a quarter to eight.'

Now the lights in the auditorium were dimming and the audience and orchestra were silent. The conductor emerged through a side-door below the stage and applause began. In the twenty-nine hours since Rosalie had left the hospital, anything could have happened. . .

And then, just as the haunting sounds of the overture began to swell, she felt a movement beside her in the darkness and he was there, muttering apologies as he pushed past three sets of strange knees to reach his seat. 'Sorry,' was all he had time to say to Rosalie, and even this drew an impatient 'sh!' from the row behind them.

A short while later the curtain rose and the ballet began. Aware of Daniel beside her as she always was, Rosalie none the less became quickly immersed. It was the Australian Ballet Company on tour, and their production of the classic was poignant and mesmerising. Then she became aware that a weight was settling on to her shoulder and she felt the soft tickle of Daniel's black hair. At first she nestled against him, her insides churning with a familiar, dangerous and very delightful warmth. . .then she realised that this wasn't a romantic moment. The cardiologist was asleep!

He's as bored as that already? was her first horrified thought, spoiling the spectacle before her. He hates ballet and he only got the tickets for my sake. . .!

No, much more likely that he had had a long day at the hospital. She relaxed again and settled herself lower in her seat so that he would be more comfortable. Afraid of waking him, she moved very gently, but he didn't stir. . .

'Wha——? What? Where. . .?' With a jerk he was awake as the house lights came on and loud applause signalled the end of the first act. He sat bolt upright, rubbed his eyes and blinked in the sudden light.

Rosalie took her first look at him this evening and saw the reddened eyes and the pale, creased face. 'Daniel! What have you been doing? You're exhausted!'

'Am I? Yes. I didn't think I was, but you're right. Did I sleep through the whole thing?'

'The first act, yes. You should have paged me here at the box office to say you couldn't make it. I would have understood.'

'Don't be ridiculous! I couldn't stand you up like that for the sake of a little fatigue.' There was the nuance of a caress in his tone as he shook his head impatiently, and she didn't press the point. In fact, she felt absurdly pleased that he seemed to value the evening in her company so highly, although it was probably his innate courtesy as much as anything else that had dictated his response.

'But what is it?' she asked now. 'What's kept you from sleep? Something at the hospital, obviously.'

'Lord, you don't know, do you? You were off at three yesterday.'

'Daniel. . .'

'Jackie's heart. . .' he explained in a confidential tone as people filled the aisles.

'Oh, *no*!' The young girl's heart function had been deteriorating steadily over the past two weeks and she had been moved to the Cardiac Intensive Care Unit a few days ago. Rosalie had visited her there each day, talking quietly to the CICU nurses afterwards and agreeing with them that things did not look good.

'No!' Daniel broke in, his energy returning. 'Her *new* heart!'

Now she saw that beneath his obvious exhaustion there was exhilaration as well. 'Then. . .?'

'Yes. It's been a long twenty-four hours. No, thirty hours. It must have started just after you left yesterday.'

'I wish someone had called.'

'No, there was no need for you to exhaust yourself as well. We had word that a heart would soon be available, but meantime Jackie's condition was worsening by the hour. I had to pull out all the stops to keep her in a fit state for surgery, and even now there may have been some kidney damage. Her heart just wasn't pumping enough blood through there by the end. Finally, at about eleven this morning, we got the heart.'

'Where did it come from?'

'Locally. So there was no dramatic flight to retrieve it from two hundred miles away as there so often is, no danger of it being on ice too long. Just a quick ambulance trip across town.'

'A road accident victim?'

'No.' His face fell into sombre lines now. 'A playground accident. A mentally handicapped boy. Middle child in a family of five. His mother turned her head, he climbed too high on some equipment and fell.'

Rosalie took in a hissing breath. 'That's terrible. . .'

'I know. But his parents were very keen to consent to organ donation, and I think it'll help them a little in their grief. People usually find it does. His corneas went to London and his kidneys to Portsmouth and Southampton.'

'Don't, Daniel! You make it sound like sending a few parcels.'

'Hey!' Suddenly he was firm, almost fierce, and he held her gaze commandingly with his black eyes. 'You must *not* look at this the wrong way around, Rosalie! That boy would have died anyway, and before transplant surgery three other kids would have died along with him — our Jackie, and the two teenagers who have his kidneys now. If what we're about is saving lives, then it *has* to be better this way!'

She was silent and helpless as he continued to study her, his eyes narrowed now, then at last she said on a wrenching sigh, 'You're right. Of course you're right.'

'Good. I'm glad you agree.' He slumped down in his seat again and rubbed at his tired face with hands that trembled a little.

'So you were on stand-by during the surgery?'

'Yes. Not needed much, fortunately. It all went smoothly, she's back in CICU and her medication is fairly standard for the next couple of days. Steroids to suppress the immune system, antibiotics to prevent infection, dopamine to improve the blood flow to the kidneys and something to pep up her heart-rate a little.'

'Again to improve the blood flow?'

'Yes. You know this stuff, don't you?'

'I'm still learning.'

'Isn't everyone?' It came out a little hollowly, then he added, 'I'll go back to the hospital after this for a final check on her.'

She didn't try to argue against the plan, although when she saw those aching eyes of his she wanted to. For a heart specialist, particularly in the still so new area of transplants, work won over sleep hands down. She did suggest, though, that she let her drive him to St Bede's in his car, since she didn't have her own, and as the next act of the ballet began he reluctantly agreed.

This time, she could tell that he was determined for politeness' sake to keep awake, and for a good while he managed it, but finally as the lights dimmed to blue-white tones for a night scene his head fell forward again and she gently put her arm around him, guided his head on to her shoulder, and left it there. In the darkness, watching the pale shapes moving so gracefully on the stage, she had to smile. Poor Daniel!

Then a deep, warm well of tenderness rose in her, very different from the rolling heat of her sensual response to him but just as powerful and just as disturbing. His breathing was slow and rhythmic, and it massaged her arm and torso in long, gentle waves where his body rested against her. In some ways at this moment he was as vulnerable and abandoned as a child, yet the weight of him was so undeniably manly, as was the reason for his fatigue — he had been battling against death itself, and she knew he had played down the drama of the past hours in his quickly sketched description.

I'll never be able to hear this music again without thinking of him, she realised as she felt the soft brush of his hair across her jawline. No matter what happens . . .or doesn't happen. . .between us in the future, there'll always be this memory. And she didn't know if this was a comforting realisation or a terrible one.

As the ballet ended, he stirred, and by the time the lights brightened during endless rounds of applause he was able to give a credible imitation of being awake. He caught her smile, though, as he pressed the back of his hand to his mouth to hide a yawn and said with a crooked smile of embarrassment, 'Sorry. Did I spoil it for you?'

'Not at all,' she answered truthfully, wishing the music and movement could continue for another hour so that the black head could fall back against her breast again. 'But I'm afraid for you it must have been——'

'I absorbed it subliminally,' he answered, deadpan. 'My subconscious loved every minute of it.'

They were silent as they walked to the car park, and she didn't try to tire him any further by demanding sparkling conversation. When they reached the low-slung white car, she gently took his car keys from him and he didn't protest, sleeping again as she drove carefully and competently to the hospital.

'Are you going to come in?' he asked as their feet made two patterns of rhythmic sound on the gritty asphalt of the quiet car park. 'She's in Isolation. . .'

'I'll have a look through the window.'

'Yes, no need to go through all the bother of putting on cap and mask and gown.'

'I was thinking more that there mightn't be room for me—with a nurse, and all that equipment, and her mother might be there as well.'

'Mm. . .' He nodded absently, and she could tell that his mind was already on his patient.

His pace quickened till she had to lengthen her own stride considerably to keep up. They reached the lift and he waited for it impatiently. She could guess at the dozens of tiny details and questions that were passing through his mind. So many things could go wrong. Infection, kidney failure, rejection. The latter was still the most dangerous possibility.

When they arrived at the isolation-room that was part of a small annexe to the Cardiac Intensive Care Unit, he left her at the window that offered a view of the room and put on with practised fluidity the sterile gown and accessories that awaited him in a tiny ante-room. In most cases when a patient was isolated like this, it was to prevent infection from getting out. With a transplant patient, however, infection coming in was the danger, and precautions were stringent. No one was allowed to see Jackie without wearing these sterile garments, as the immuno-suppressants that prevented her body's rejection of its new heart also lowered her resistance to infection as well.

Rosalie was able to watch Daniel as he hovered over his patient, although through the double thickness of glass she could hear nothing. Mrs Rogerson was there, dozing until the new arrival woke her, and a nurse was keeping constant vigil as well. Jackie was still attached to a ventilator, an intravenous drip, drains, catheter and an ECG machine. Engulfed in all this equipment, she looked fragile and lifeless, but Rosalie could see that the red-haired nurse — Jenny Lucas was her name, but Rosalie didn't know her very well — was smiling and looking quite happy as she answered a barrage of questions from the doctor. Mrs Rogerson had questions too, and Daniel answered them with soothing gestures. He flipped through Jackie's charts, his eyes narrowing as he assessed the detailed pattern of measurements plotted there — temperature, pulse, blood-pressure. . .the list went on.

It's like a silent film or a mimed play, Rosalie thought as she watched, remembering the much larger stage she had been watching this evening. And Daniel Canaday was so well cast as a doctor, too. The blue hospital gown, cap, mask, gloves and slippers didn't look ridiculous on him as they did on so many people, probably because he was so used to wearing them that he didn't think about them.

He spent about fifteen minutes with Jackie, but Rosalie wasn't bored. Mrs Rogerson caught sight of her through the glass and smiled tiredly, then Jenny Lucas gave a comradely wave. Daniel didn't look at her at all. He was standing quite quietly now, simply watching his patient with a searching, almost tender expression that nearly brought tears to Rosalie's eyes.

He doesn't want to leave, she realised. He'd sit there all night if there was the slightest excuse to. He's watching her face because he wants her to *tell* him that she's going to be all right. Rosalie had done the same thing with critically ill patients of her own.

Finally, after some reassuring words to Mrs Rogerson, he left the isolation-room, flinging his gown and its accessories into a bin as he emerged and caught sight of Rosalie. 'You've been at this window the whole time?'

'Mm-hmm.'

He smiled, understanding why she hadn't gone off in search of a seat and a magazine. It's nice not to have to explain, she thought.

'She's doing fine,' he said now. 'Too soon to tell how she'll do in the long term, of course, but no problem signs at all yet. We'll wean her off the ventilator tomorrow, take that tube out of her throat and she'll be able to talk.'

'I don't suppose she'll want to say much.'

'No, and fortunately she probably won't remember much of these first few days later on.'

Reaching the car, they again drove in silence and Rosalie could see out of the corner of her eye that it was an effort for him to stay awake to direct her to his house. She was finding his weariness contagious and wasn't thinking very clearly — or was it just that he was filling her thoughts, leaving room for little else? — so it wasn't until they turned into his street that she realised she herself would have to take a taxi home.

But Daniel had his own very firm ideas on the subject. 'No! Stay the night! What shift do you have tomorrow? An afternoon? Plenty of time to get home tomorrow, then. My spare-room bed is all made up.'

'No, I —— ' she began nervously.

'Listen!' He turned to her, his black eyes and fatigue-creased face betraying impatience. 'If you're worried about the impropriety of it I promise you I'm far too tired to even think about. . .'

He trailed off because suddenly they both *were* thinking about the attraction that flared between them, and Rosalie was thinking frantically, I *must* go home. Then he had thrown open the car door and climbed out, and she had to hurry to pull the car keys from the ignition and follow him. 'I want to be at the hospital by six,' he said, his voice completely businesslike now. 'I *have* to get some sleep, so let's not argue about this. Please!'

She could see that it would be cruel to protest any further. Clearly, tonight at least, he was making no attempt at seduction. Thinking longingly of bed herself, she followed him up the stone steps. Once inside, however, she found that he was offering her hot chocolate and wouldn't take no for an answer, so they sat in the kitchen while he heated milk for her and drank a long glass of cold water himself.

'I like your place,' she said tentatively as he thrust a steaming mug towards her. She knew he didn't want to talk much.

But he answered cheerfully enough, 'Thanks,' as he poured himself another glass of water.

This house was an old Victorian mansion, subdivided now into four generous flats, and his contained the original kitchen, huge enough to seat a banquet as well as to cook one, but modernised and made almost as comfortable as a sitting-room. There was a Persian rug on the tiled floor, and bookcases and potted plants broke up the space. Everywhere, she saw quirky but very pleasing touches of decoration that she assumed must be the work of his sister Amanda — an oriental tapestry, an antique cash register with its grainy wood lovingly restored to a glossy sheen, a collection of carved and painted wooden fruits of all shapes and sizes arranged in a large wooden bowl.

'You were right about your sister,' she said impulsively, waving her hand to take in the room as well as the wide passage they had come along from the big front door and vestibule. 'She does have a marvellous eye for the unusual.'

'Amanda?' he queried, amused. 'I'll take that as a
compliment, but I don't think she would. All this stuff
is my idea of decoration. She likes a more formal
approach.'

'Oh!' Rosalie laughed. 'Well, I'm sure I'd like that
too, but ——' She broke off, suddenly flustered. She
had been about to say something about his taste
matching hers, and it occurred to her that the wording
of the comment might sound a little provocative at this
time of night, alone in his flat. He was looking at her,
his large glass of water poised halfway to his lips, and
his eyebrows were raised quizzically. She finished
hastily, 'But, since I don't have any professional training in art or design, my opinion wouldn't matter to
her.'

'Oh, I think it might. . .' he replied softly, and she
didn't know what to make of that at all.

Fifteen minutes later she was enfolded in clean,
delicately floral-patterned sheets that smelled faintly
of lavender. Daniel, after uttering scarcely three more
words to her and smiling wryly at her as he said
goodnight, had retired to his own room. She knew
what the smile meant. They were both aware that if he
hadn't been so tired her spending the night here would
have been far too dangerous.

It's dangerous anyway, she thought feverishly as she
waited for sleep. It's all happening far too fast.

'Are you going to that meeting about the heart care
project?' Beverly Moore said to Rosalie on Tuesday
afternoon at the end of their shift together.

'I certainly am,' the senior nurse replied. 'I've been
interested in the idea of community outreach since the
project was first talked about. In fact, I suspect I'll end
up volunteering for the committee!' Rosalie finished a
little ruefully. She knew from experience that such
things could mushroom into a very heavy commitment.

'I've been thinking the same thing,' Beverly was

saying. Stocky, dark-haired and in her late twenties, the more junior nurse was very ambitious and had been taking evening classes in health administration for nearly two years. 'That kind of thing is always good experience and looks impressive on a curriculum vitae.'

'Then we may be rivals for the position of chair,' Rosalie teased.

'Chair? Hardly! Oh, you're joking. But anyway, I'm sure there'll be room on the committee for both of us. The meeting's at six. Are you going home?'

'No, it hardly seems worth it,' Rosalie answered. 'We're a bit late finishing here, so I'll just stay on in town.'

'Same here,' Beverly said. 'Want to grab coffee and a snack together to fill the time?'

'Oh. . .that would be nice, but—um—I have some shopping I need to do.' Trying to control her rising colour, Rosalie was very aware that this was not the truth. Daniel had already asked her this morning to go for coffee with him.

'OK,' the younger nurse shrugged equably, unaware that Rosalie was fibbing. 'See you at six, then.'

'Yes.'

Beverly hurried off while Rosalie played with her bag for a few moments to give the other nurse a head start. She was supposed to be meeting Daniel at his car in ten minutes—just enough time to stop in the Ladies' room on the way out to change into the dark green-toned Paisley dress of brushed cotton that she had brought with her this morning in a carrier bag.

But when she got to Daniel's low-slung white car she found a note—addressed only to 'R'—tucked under the windscreen-wiper and going slightly limp under the influence of a mild June drizzle that had begun to fall. 'Can't make it. Something's come up. Sorry. D,' was all it said, but it cast her into such a state of disappointment that she went numbly in the

direction of the café he had mentioned—it was a
fifteen-minute walk—without even putting up her
umbrella, let alone thinking to take her own car that
had been parked in the hospital car park just fifty
metres from his own all day.

How ridiculous to mind so much, she scolded herself. *It's a medical emergency on some other ward, no
doubt, and I might have known it would happen. As
long as it's nothing to do with Jackie Billings, though.
I'll see him in two hours anyway, and. . .*

But it was no good. The acute disappointment
remained, reminding Rosalie not for the first time how
dangerously deep were the currents of her attraction
to the young cardiologist. Forcing herself to stop
thinking about him, she found a newspaper that a
previous customer had left unnoticed on the next seat
and began to read it after ordering cappuccino and
carrot cake.

An instinct to look up each time the door opened
would not go away, however, and when it happened
for the third time she was confronted by the sight of
Beverly Moore. Their eyes met for a moment, then
Rosalie lifted the newspaper in front of her face in a
pointless and incriminating gesture of concealment.
Now it looked as if she had declined Bev's invitation
because she didn't like the other woman.

She just had time to see a cold, pained look come
over the ambitious junior's face before the nurse
stepped quickly back out of the café, shut the door
sharply and hurried off down the wet, glistening street.

'Oh, hell!' Rosalie muttered under her breath. 'How
stupid of me!'

Stupid to have told the white lie to Beverly in the
first place, stupid to have come here alone, and very
stupid to have tried to hide. It was impossible to follow
Beverly and explain. She was halfway through her
coffee and cake and her bill was unpaid. Beverly would
be lost in the five o'clock crowds by now.

'Hell!' Rosalie said again.

The only way to retrieve the situation was to collar Bev before the meeting and admit the truth, and fortunately she managed to do this.

'I'm sorry about this afternoon,' she said in a low tone as she slipped into an uncomfortable orange plastic seat beside the other nurse an hour or so later, in a conference-room in the very depths of the hospital. 'I was supposed to meet someone. I should have told you straight away. In fact, I don't know why I didn't.' She was blushing and she wasn't doing this very well, but Beverly's distant attention was softening into a more receptive attitude now.

'Someone special?' she asked.

'I—I don't know yet. Anyway, he cancelled at the last minute, and if I'd been more on the ball I'd have hauled you into that café and we could have had a nice chat after all. I'm sorry I acted in such a silly way.'

'I understand,' Beverly answered carefully. 'I suppose it's someone from the hospital, is it? The man who cancelled?'

'Yes,' Rosalie admitted reluctantly.

'That always makes it awkward. Let's forget the whole thing.'

She seemed to do this without effort, but Rosalie found that she still felt uncomfortable, and wished that the meeting weren't taking place tonight after all. She heard Daniel's voice behind her and then he went on up to the front of the room, still in conversation with Max Hillston. Several more people trickled in, including Heather Barry, the hospital's co-ordinator of volunteer services, who was tireless in her involvement with any new community programme. She was another candidate for the heart care committee, Rosalie felt sure.

'Let's all gather round here at the front,' Daniel Canaday said several minutes later. 'I don't think anyone else is coming. I was only expecting this sort of turn-out.'

'Yes, why they gave us this huge room I don't know,' Max Hillston came in.

So Rosalie and Beverly, who had seated themselves further back in the rows of orange chairs, came forward, as did one or two others, and the meeting took place in a loosely grouped circle. Daniel was clearly the energy behind the project. It was typical, Rosalie thought, that within a month of his arrival Dr Canaday should have got the thing off the ground in the face of daunting bureaucratic dilly-dallying. There was still a long way to go, though.

'Basically, we have no money at this stage,' the cardiologist was saying. 'But we won't get any unless we form a committee and find ways to go out and interest people and organisations in what we're doing. The local council is keen in theory—in fact, I was hoping someone from there might turn up tonight, but he hasn't—but they won't commit themselves until they see that we can create something that's attractive and interesting to the public. If we get that sort of seed money, other organisations should start to chip in.'

An hour was spent in talking about other ideas for fund-raising, as well as the immediate tasks ahead of the committee, and then it was decided that the time had come to actually elect that committee. It was clear already that Daniel Canaday would chair it. 'And I thought four more people,' he said. 'Five is a nice number. Bigger than that and it gets unwieldy, splits into factions, wastes a lot of time on procedure. I'm not big on procedure,' he grinned rather wickedly, and several people laughed.

Rosalie herself hadn't said much as yet, apart from contributing a couple of quiet ideas that had been well-received and noted down by Heather Barry, who was acting as minutes-taker for this evening.

'Five sounds good to me,' Max Hillston said. 'But

I'm not going to be one of them, I'm afraid. I just haven't the time, although I'd like to be involved in other ways.'

'Who *is* interested, then?' Daniel asked, and his eyes flicked questioningly around the room, seeming to skate over Rosalie's own brown-eyed gaze as they had done for the entire meeting.

She had been hoping, against her better judgement, for one of those sizzling locked glances, but it hadn't happened. Had he really been called to an emergency this afternoon?

'I think we need a secretary, obviously, and some-one to manage the books—supposing we do get some money eventually—and then just a couple of floating people to do whatever else comes up.'

'I'd be very happy to be treasurer,' an older man offered.

He had spoken frequently earlier, and Rosalie knew that he was Jim Paulson, a recovered heart-attack patient who had become very committed to the idea of increasing public awareness about risk and prevention. In addition, it appeared that he had important business interests in the area and could well be a good source of contacts for fund-raising. Heather Barry put herself forward as secretary, which was also met with general approval.

'I'd like to be one of the floating members,' Mrs Paulson then said, and it turned out that she had a wide experience on charity committees and was, like her husband, in touch with many useful contacts.

'That leaves one more,' Daniel Canaday said, and there was a pause.

Finally Rosalie and Beverly both spoke together.

'I'd like to.'

'I'll volunteer.'

'Hmm. Two of you,' Daniel frowned, and at last Rosalie caught a glance directed at herself. But it didn't contain the private glimmer of awareness that

she expected. . .yes, and wanted now. Instead, his
dark eyes were narrowed and a definite warning
gleamed through those long lashes.

I don't want you on the committee, Rosalie Crane.
He didn't say the words aloud, but he might as well
have done. The meaning in that glance was remarkably
clear.

'Perhaps this calls for a written ballot, then,' Jim
Paulson was saying. 'And, with all due respect, Dr
Canaday, I think we should have one anyway,' the
businessman went on. 'I know we don't want to get
bogged down in procedure, but I think it should be on
record that this committee was duly and properly
elected. If we do start to have substantial funds to
manage later on. . .'

'I agree,' Daniel came in suddenly and surprisingly.
'Yes. Good point. I suggest we break for coffee, then,
while. . . Heather?'

'Yes,' the volunteer co-ordinator nodded. 'I can
easily type up a ballot form with all the names and
positions and run it off on the photocopier in my
office. It'll only take five minutes.'

'Good. And meanwhile coffee and tea are available
in the kitchenette at the back of this room, everyone,'
Daniel said. 'Help yourselves.'

Rosalie stood up, needing a cup of tea suddenly,
and Beverly turned to her. 'Rivals!' she laughed.

Rosalie managed a smile. 'Not serious ones. I really
don't mind either way. We've both got the same sorts
of things to offer.'

'And we'd both do a good job,' Beverly agreed, but,
remembering what the junior nurse had said about her
career earlier today, Rosalie thought that perhaps she
was hoping to win.

They separated and Rosalie headed for the kitchenette, where steam issued in clouds from a rapidly
boiling urn. Joy Paulson was there, dispensing teas
and coffees, and Rosalie hesitated in the doorway,

wanting to wait until the small crush had subsided. Before she could move into the tiny room, however, she felt a hand gripping her upper arm and a low voice behind her said, 'I need to see you.'

No need to wonder who it was. A moment later, Daniel Canaday had pulled her into the smaller meeting-room just along the corridor and had kicked the door closed behind them so that they were in a ghostly darkness of ranged chairs lit only by light seeping under the door and around the closed hatch of the servery window that connected this room with the kitchenette.

'I don't want you on that committee, Rosalie,' he growled. In the darkness, she could see that he was frowning and tense. Was he angry?

'Why not?' she demanded.

'Oh, surely——! No. There isn't time now and anyway. . .' He glanced towards the rectangle of light spilling from the servery hatch. The sound of laughter and voices came clearly through, which meant that they, in turn, could be overheard easily. 'Damn it! You *must* know why! Meet me afterwards. Stay behind. I'm locking up. Everyone else will have gone. We can talk then. Just withdraw your name, Rosalie!'

He left the room without giving her a chance to reply. She stayed on, standing in the reaching fan of light that came through the now open door from the corridor. There were no more voices coming through the closed servery hatch now. Everyone had taken their coffee and tea and gone.

Belatedly, Rosalie went and poured a cup for herself as Daniel's ultimatum echoed in her ears. 'Just withdraw your name. . .' She had no time to wonder why he felt so strongly about it. She simply had to decide whether to obey what was virtually an order. For a moment, as a gulp of too hot tea seared her throat, she thought, No! I won't withdraw! Let it be put to the vote! Then, and she didn't know if it was out of weakness or strength, she decided to do as he wanted.

And so each member of the new committee was elected unopposed and the meeting was concluded. After congratulating Beverly, and still feeling ravaged by the whole confusing episode, Rosalie waited in the nearby Ladies' room until she was sure everyone would have left. She had had half a mind not to wait for Daniel as he had suggested — or commanded — but that seemed unfair, and if he had an explanation she wanted to hear it.

She found him locking up the kitchenette.

'There's supposed to be another meeting in here at eight,' he said, 'but I was told to lock up, so. . .'

'Why didn't you want me on the committee, Daniel?' Rosalie came in, on a low note. She wasn't prepared now to waste time in small talk. He turned to her, the ring of hospital keys gripped tightly in his hand.

'Do you really not know?'

'No, I don't.'

And then he had crossed the space between them and pulled her urgently into his arms, pressing his lips to hers hungrily. 'Because of this, of course,' he said huskily. 'It's bad enough seeing you on the ward, but at least we're both so busy there I can manage to resist you. But some of those committee meetings will be dull as ditch-water. How on earth can I keep my mind on the heart care project — which is *important* — when I'm just sitting there wanting you? *Wanting* you so badly, and wishing I could just take you by the hand and go! God, Rosalie!'

She felt the heat of him beginning to seep into her and crumble any defences she might have had left, and she heard herself saying against his lips and against his hair, 'I suppose I wanted to be on the committee. . . partly because I knew I'd see you.'

It was a horribly naked confession, and she wished,

even as she spoke, that she hadn't made it, but he only laughed softly and caught her lips again before murmuring, 'But that's not how we want to see each other, is it?' He mimicked primly, 'Dr Canaday, chair, and Sister Crane, general member. And shall we read the minutes now, please —— ?' He broke off and continued searingly, 'I want to have you alone, somewhere where we can. . .'

He didn't finish. He didn't need to. Rosalie took in a ragged breath that matched his own and then they were locked helplessly together, her tender breasts, alive with sensation, crushed hotly against his chest and his hips moulded into her own.

'Don't you agree now,' he breathed at last, 'how impossible it would be, with this thing happening between us?'

'Yes,' she admitted raggedly. 'Yes.'

'Can you think of anything worse?'

'No. . .' And then, suddenly, she could. 'Unless. . . if it ends. . .'

'If it ends?' he echoed, drawing slightly away from her as they both heard voices coming down the stairs at the end of the corridor. 'Yes, that could well be worse.'

CHAPTER FIVE

FOR the first time, Rosalie had turned down Howard's invitation for Friday night. She had used a ridiculous excuse, too — that she had an aunt who had invited her to tea — and now she was guiltily petrified about being found out.

I've gone quite giddy over Daniel, she said to herself as she drove in to work, adding firmly and quite futilely, It's got to stop!

It was Friday morning, and she would be seeing him tonight — which was, of course, why she had refused Howard, and she knew she shouldn't have done it. I'll tell Daniel I can't make it after all, she decided distractedly.

He arrived about an hour after she herself had started work, and they met up over the bed of one of the men who was due for the exploratory process of cardiac catheterisation.

Mr Thompson had spent a restless night and turned with a worried expression to Rosalie as soon as she entered the room. 'It's not today, that catheter thing, is it?'

'No, Mr Thompson, it's Monday.'

'I was having a lot of pain during the night.'

'Yes, Night Sister told me you were restless. The nitroglycerine didn't help?'

'It gives me such a headache. Worse than the chest pain. I stopped those pills that go under the tongue. But it wasn't the pain so much as. . .this catheter-whatsit. That probably means I'm going to have a bypass next, doesn't it?'

'You'll have to ask——'

'Me,' Daniel Canaday supplied at that moment,

94

approaching the bed with an energetic grin. 'But I missed the question.'

Over the anxious patient's bed he took the time to telegraph a brief, private glance to Rosalie that made her suddenly freshly conscious that sunshine was streaming through the window and birds were almost drowning the sounds of traffic outside with their singing. Wondering if she was being weak, she decided not to cancel tonight after all.

'Mr Thompson is a little concerned about the cardiac catheterisation and its implications,' Rosalie explained, bending her thoughts firmly to her patient.

'I was going to come and talk to you about that this afternoon, Mr Thompson,' Dr Canaday said, 'But I can take the time now, if you'd rather.'

'Well, not if you're busy. . .'

'Mr Thompson was too anxious about it to sleep, Dr Canaday,' Rosalie came in clearly. 'Don't be shy about asking, Mr Thompson. If something is worrying you, the doctor can talk to you now. Cardiologists might be busy, and they definitely like you to know that they're important. . .but they're not gods!' she finished wickedly, and darted a cheeky glance at the particular cardiologist who was present at the moment.

He raised his eyebrows in mock-disapproval then lapsed into a chuckle that ought to reassure his patient that he was indeed human. Rosalie left him sitting by Mr Thompson's bed, and crossed the small room to her next patient, who also needed to speak his mind, it seemed.

'It's the food, Nurse,' he rasped, through a throat that had been seared by a lifetime of heavy smoking. 'It doesn't agree with me.'

'Are you having stomach pains?' Rosalie queried, concerned. Old Mr Fenstowe was irascible but not very strong, and pain that he attributed to disgestive problems might mean something more serious.

But it appeared that pain was not the problem.

'It's not that. . . It's just. . . That stuff last night. . .'

'Yes?' Rosalie frantically tried to think what had been on the menu, but of course after seeing so many meals wheeled through the ward over the years she didn't bother to keep track of an area that was more the province of a dietician than a nurse.

'It was *rice*, but it wasn't pudding, you follow? It wasn't *sweet*, and the rice was *brown*. I couldn't get used to it.'

'Oh, it was rice pilaf?'

'Yes, that was it. Rice pea-laugh. I didn't know you could have *savoury* rice.'

'If you didn't like it. . .'

'Well, it wasn't that I didn't *like* it, I just couldn't get *used* to it, if you know what I mean.'

'I think so,' Rosalie answered, suppressing an impatient sigh, then she said to him placatingly, 'I'll see what I can do, Mr Fenstowe,' and the old man settled back into his bed, apparently satisfied.

Perhaps he had just wanted a chat, and this was his way of earning one. She decided not to speak to the dietician about his menu at this stage. He might decide that he liked 'rice pea-laugh' and if Mrs Fenstowe could be induced to follow the recipe for it in the booklet of healthy, low-cholesterol-cooking ideas that all coronary patients were given on discharge it would do both him and his wife more good than the fatty chips they no doubt ate several times a week. Rice pilaf was certainly healthier than rice pudding, as well.

Rosalie laughed at herself as she left the room. Daniel was still talking rather earnestly to Mr Thompson, and listening very earnestly as well. . . Mr Fenstowe was an old sweetie, really, and she ought not to feel irritated by the fact that his diet obviously came straight out of a cardiologist's nightmare.

That's why this heart care project is so important, if we can really get it working, she realised. If there are still people like Mr Fenstowe who don't even *know*

that you can eat brown rice plainly steamed or flavoured with herbs instead of white rice stuck in a
gluggy, sickly pudding loaded with jam and cream and
eggs. . .

Then she remembered that she wasn't on the heart
care project committee and why, and she stopped
noticing the birds and kept hearing instead that calm
agreement of Daniel's ten days ago. 'If it ends. . .'
Drawing a deep, careful breath, she refused to listen
to those ominous words in her head and went into the
next room to continue checking on her patients.

And somehow she must have ducked into the store-
room or the nurses' station at the wrong moment,
because she didn't encounter Dr Canaday again on his
round and missed seeing him as he left the ward. It
wasn't until after lunch that she saw him again, and
then he was too busy to be anything but businesslike.

'Have to go up and see Jackie Billings and I'm
running late,' he said as he stopped at the nurses'
station on his way into the ward. The young transplant
patient continued to do well and would eventually be
ready to return to this ward, with its less intensive
level of care. 'Just wanted to fill you in on Mr
Thompson before I chat to those other two cath
patients. I think we've all been assuming that he was a
strong candidate for bypass, but now I'm not so sure.
He's very against the idea, and seems highly motivated
to change his lifestyle and work on a non-surgical
approach. All depends on what the procedure reveals
on Monday, of course, but I'm prepared for a bit of a
fight with Trevalley over the issue.'

He narrowed his eyes for a fraction of a second and
flicked a tiny glance at Rosalie as he spoke the senior
surgeon's name, as if warily expecting her to be on the
older man's side. They were both reluctant to bring up
his name with each other, to tell the truth.

Rosalie said carefully, 'He does tend to favour the
surgical approach. I think he feels that some patients

can overestimate their ability to stick to a demanding programme of medication, as well as the lifestyle changes that we ask of all our patients.'

'Partly that,' Daniel agreed. 'Partly it's just that he's a born surgeon. . . Mostly,' he added, his voice dropping low, 'he's a typical Type A personality. Wants to get in there with something quick and drastic and fix the problem *now*.'

'And of course there's nothing of the Type A about you, Doctor,' Rosalie murmured with deceptive mildness.

He looked at her for a moment and she was surprised to see that he seemed angry. Surely she hadn't hit a raw nerve with that last teasing comment?

'What's the matter, Daniel?' she asked in a low tone.

'Nothing,' he shrugged impatiently. 'It shouldn't be a contest between Trevalley and me. . . Should it?'

'No, it shouldn't'. She met his probing gaze steadily and her answer was firm. The only problem was, she realised as he strode away, she didn't know if he meant a contest over Mr Thompson's case, or over herself.

Would he still be angry tonight, just hours away, when he came to the cottage to pick her up for their evening together? she wondered. At home, when it came time to dress, she found that she was quite nervous and tense — guilty, because she had turned down Howard? Afraid of Daniel's mood? Simply eager to see him? She didn't know.

Impulsively, she decided to take a bath instead of a shower. It did seem to help. She felt cooler and calmer as she pulled the rust-coloured taffeta dress from her wardrobe and slipped it over her head and shoulders so that it fell snugly against her skin, and against the silky briefs and boned strapless bra that were all she could wear beneath it.

But is it too much? she wondered, as she put on make-up and accessories, and brushed her hair into a lustrous halo. Does it make me look. . .too eager for him? When she had worn the dress for Howard, that hadn't seemed to matter, and she had not felt this heightened awareness of her own sensuality.

Nervously, she tried to pull at the pretty necklike of the dress so that it covered more of her white shoulders and hid the lavish pale mounds of her breasts. It was no good. The dress fitted exactly as it was meant to, in only one way, and if she tried to pull it up she ruined the fall of the fabric around her shoulders and it looked ludicrous.

I'll change, she decided desperately, but at that moment the doorbell pealed and in a panic she ran down to him, her nervousness swamped by anticipation as she crossed the front hall so that she arrived breathless, flushed and smiling.

He had brought flowers — creamy roses, white carnations and pale, delicate lilies in an informal glowing bunch that contrasted sharply with the dark suit he wore, and with the dark hair that curled on his neck and those passionate, black eyes. She didn't have to ask him if he liked the dress. The suppressed gasp and momentary flaring of his pupils told her that.

'They're beautiful,' she said, taking the flowers and burying her face in the scent of the roses in an attempt to slow the frantic beating of her heart.

'May I come in and help you arrange them?' he said in a low, throaty tone, and they both knew that once he was inside the door the lovely flowers would be forgotten.

They were. As she walked distractedly into the living-room in hazy search of a vase, he coaxed the flowers from her grasp and laid them on the coffee-table then turned her wordlessly into his arms, running his fingers through her hair then stroking the bare, silky skin of her neck and shoulders. She lifted her chin willingly to meet his kiss and tasted the familiar, almost salty freshness of his mouth. His lips were as hungry as hers, and minutes passed as they explored each sensitive fragment of their parted mouths.

Gradually, as Rosalie was carried along on an eager tide of pleasure and discovery, Daniel's touch grew more urgent and his body more demanding as it pressed against her soft curves. He caressed the pale shape of her shoulders then ran fluting fingers along the wide, low neckline of her dress to brush at the tantalising slopes of her breasts. Moments later, she gasped as he coaxed the rustling silk taffeta further from her shoulders, then she gasped again and a throaty moan escaped from deep within her.

Somehow the fragile hooks of her bra had come unfastened and suddenly her breasts had sprung free and spilled generously into his cupped hands, which soon caressed the searingly sensitive tips of the full globes into sizzling awareness. Before she could draw breath again, he had swept her off her feet and plunged her into the deep comfort of the long couch before stretching lion-like on top of her and finding her mouth again so that locks of his dark hair brushed her forehead.

Shuddering, she arched her back and pressed her swollen breasts against him, hungry for the touch of his bare skin against her own. But her fingers, plucking at the stubborn buttons of his cream shirt, were coaxed gently aside.

'Let *me* finish first,' he whispered. 'Oh, Rosalie, I've wanted this. . .!'

Caressingly, he slipped the taffeta down to her waist — her bra had already been tossed aside — so that her entire torso lay naked to his hungry gaze. Carefully controlling his ragged breathing, he moulded the curves of her surprisingly small waist with his hands then slid them down so that the dress moved still lower. In another minute, she would be quite naked, then, as he had suggested, it would be her turn to slip his clothes from his body in the same eager, caressing way. After that. . .

'No, Daniel stop!' she breathed at last, just as fingers had begun to play at the lace-edged waist of her silky briefs.

'No?' she felt his immediate stiffening.

'Not here.'

'You mean. . .upstairs?' he growled.

'No. . . I think. . . I mean. . .not yet.'

There was a silence while she heard her hesitant words ringing in the air. Did she wish them unspoken?

Daniel Canaday had the same question. 'Are you sure? Do you mean that?'

'Yes.' She forced firmness into her tone as reason and doubt struggled with a tide of physical need stronger than she had ever felt before.

'All right,' he answered, slowly and neutrally.

Relieved — and aching with regret — she struggled to sit up in order to recapture her dress, and as she reached for the luxurious fabric her breasts fell heavily forward and brushed against his shirt, searing their tips instantly into hard stones of desire once again. A ragged sigh of surrender escaped her and instinctively she sought to nuzzle her face against his neck, but he pulled away and pressed a crushed handful of taffeta up to her collarbone.

'No, Rosalie,' he said through clenched teeth. 'Either we stop now. . .or we *don't* stop,' and before she could answer him he had rolled in one lithe movement off the couch and on to his feet with his back to her.

As she sat up and held the twisted dress against her, he headed for the stairs, and only when he reached them did he speak.

'We have that dinner booking,' he said. 'We're late already. Better get dressed.'

'Yes. . .'

'And Rosalie. . .?'

'Hmm?'

'Don't put that gorgeous thing back on or I can't answer for what I might do.'

She didn't reply, and waited until she heard the door of the hall bathroom close abruptly behind him before lifting her own trembling limbs from the couch and forcing them to carry her upstairs. Closing her bedroom door and closeting herself in the dressing-room and bathroom that adjoined it, she still throbbed with awareness and unfulfilled desire. It would have been achingly easy to go on. . . Why had she put such an abrupt stop to it?

Because I'm a fool, she told herself bitterly. I want to hear him say he loves me first. I'm like a teenager . . .far sillier than Elise Jones. . .to have fallen for him like this so soon. It must be my hormones. . .a biological imperative, or something. Then she laughed aloud briefly. Oh, that's just as melodramatic as a teenage crush! I was right to stop it. It *can't* work!

This last was anguished but hard-edged and realisic. With a brisk gesture, she pulled a pale grey cashmere dress from her wardrobe. Long-sleeved, high-necked and knee-length, it might be a little warm for this evening although the wool was finely knitted, but it couldn't be interpreted as a provocative garment, she decided, and the shade of grey, although pretty and soft, did nothing for her unusual colouring.

Feeling intensely nervous and vulnerable, she descended the stairs again, but Daniel was nowhere to be seen. He appeared moments later, with the tendrils of black hair on his neck curling damply. He was grinning at her, too, and she met his cheerfulness with a small frown which he noticed at once.

'*I* had a cold shower,' he said. 'Didn't you?'

'No.'

'You should have done. I feel a lot better. . . although that dress is scarcely the sack I was hinting at.'

'Isn't it?'

'No. The way it hugs your luscious hips and bre——
' He broke off. 'Anyway, you'll run out of dry towels
if we don't start thinking about something else. I used
the one I found folded on that stool in the bathroom.
I hope that was all right?'

'Yes, fine,' she murmured, not sure how to respond
to this change of mood.

There was a sense of very youthful triumph about
him that she didn't share, and she couldn't understand
why he was feeling it, when she herself was wound
into a tight mass of wariness, confusion and thwarted
need.

'What's the time?' he wanted to know.

'Ten to seven.'

'We're due at seven and it's a half-hour drive. Let's
chuck the restaurant and have that picnic on the beach
instead.'

'*Picnic* on the *beach*?'

'Yes, why not? I suggested it once before, remember? Doesn't the cliff path along here lead down to a
secluded cove or two?'

'Yes, but. . .'

'I have a jacket in the car. You must have a coat.
There's still plenty of light and it's really quite warm.
We'll make a salad, take some lemon, buy fish and
chips from that place I saw on the main road a couple
of miles back. . .'

She could only nod and accept the idea, while
inwardly wondering if she should change again. Deciding against it—he was already coaxing her to the
kitchen to command her help with the salad—she tried
to enter his mood, but the more she tried, the stiffer
and more reluctant she felt. Somehow, his energy, his
openness, his zest for life frightened her tonight.

They worked in silence, washing lettuce and slicing
tomatoes, until she looked up and found that he was
studying her.

'I suppose you don't do this sort of thing with Howard?'

'No.' She couldn't help smiling a little.

'How old is Howard, do you know?'

'Fifty-three.'

'Old enough to be my father.'

'*Not* old enough to be mine.'

'Is it *still* bothering you? That I'm five years younger than you are?'

'Sometimes, yes. Quite often. . .'

'Rosalie, that's so. . . You're *impossible* sometimes, do you know that?' he said, trembling with impatience. 'You're only as old as you feel. Haven't you heard that? It's true!'

'Well, sometimes I *feel* about forty-five!' she retorted, resolutely continuing to mix oil and vinegar for a dressing, although she wanted to drop the ingredients and pace the room as he was doing.

But he refused to be put off by her words, and came to confront her. 'When you're with *me* do you feel forty-five?' he demanded intensely. '*Do* you? *Ever*?'

She was silent for a long moment, then said in a low voice, 'No, not when I'm with you, Daniel.'

He looked grimly satisfied at this admission, but some of his energy and triumph was gone now, she could see, and she thought that it would be ironic if she *did* convince him in the end that the gap between them mattered. They finished the salad, gathered plastic crockery, cutlery and napkins, found her coat and got into the car.

'A bottle of wine would be nice too, don't you think?' he suggested.

'If you like.' She had packed clear plastic picnic cups.

'Can't you at least *manufacture* some enthusiasm?' he burst out suddenly. 'Hang it, let's go to the restaurant after all.'

'No, the picnic sounds ——'

'It was an idiotic impulse. You don't want to go.
You're not dressed for it. Neither am I, if it comes to
that.'

And tersely he cut off her protests as he changed his
route to take them, after all, to the planned restaurant,
where they were now very late.

It didn't seem to matter. They were given a very
intimate table, lit by a dim yellow light that made his
tanned face glow warmly and his black eyes shimmer
darkly. There was a dark shadow on his jaw now, too,
as this morning's shave receded into the past. Afterwards, she couldn't remember what they had talked
about. She knew that he had tried to draw her out,
and had tried herself to cross the barrier that this
evening's near-consummation had thrown up between
them.

I haven't slept with a man since Mike died, she
realised during a silence towards the end of their meal.
That's a long time. And to be swept into it like this by
my own passion. . . It's too frightening.

Even as she thought this she glanced up from the
coffee Bavarian cream in front of her and saw that his
gaze was lingering on her throat and breasts as if he
wanted to taste them instead of the Bavarian cream
that he, too, had ordered.

'I was thinking,' he said softly, when he saw that she
was looking at him, 'It's a shame to let that picnic
basket and salad go to waste. It's supposed to be fine
and warm tomorrow. How about I pick you up and we
drive to Tintagel and Boscastle Harbour, do what we
planned to do tonight and pick up fish and chips for a
meal on the beach — only lunch instead of dinner?'

'Sounds wonderful,' she answered, with a lightness
that wasn't quite genuine.

'Good', he replied, but a frown hovered like an
unlucky crease on his brow and she wanted to suggest
that they plan the picnic for next week — never mind

about the salad — so that each of them had a chance to cool off and think.

She didn't, though. Instead, they left the restaurant and he drove her home. She spent the drive dreading the kiss she knew would come at the end of it — or, rather, dreading the uncontrollable tide of her own response. But when he pulled up outside her front gate he left the engine running and said softly, 'I won't come in.' The kiss that followed was almost as brief and chaste as the touch of Howard Trevalley's lips, except, since it was Daniel, she felt a trembling that could have come from herself or from him, she didn't know.

'The picnic basket,' she began huskily as he retreated back into his seat.

'Might as well leave it in my car,' he said. 'That salad will keep. Shall I pick you up at ten?'

'Sounds good.'

'Goodnight, then, Rosalie.'

'Goodnight.'

'What? *Reading* on duty, Nurse Jones?'

Daniel had come on to the ward, seen Rosalie's bright, glossy head bent over paperwork, and snatched quickly at this opportunity to distract himself with some silly chat. The student nurse, sitting at a desk on the opposite side of the nurses' station, gave him a pretty, slightly guilty and indignant smile. . .which he scarcely saw.

'I'm studying my notes,' Elise retorted. 'That's all right, isn't it? I had a moment and Sister said — '

'Of course it's all right,' Daniel returned, still light and teasing. 'A bit old-fashioned, though, don't you think? The written word?'

'You mean. . .?'

'I'd have thought a serious student like you would have found a personal coach.' The banter occupied about ten per cent of his mind. The rest was fixed on

Rosalie, who was resolutely ignoring the exchange, damn her.

'Oh!' Elise laughed. 'Private tutoring from a well-heeled young specialist, you mean?'

'Something like that.' He laughed too, and turned away.

Rosalie had looked up at last. This was the first time they had seen each other since Saturday's less than successful picnic at Tintagel, and he wanted *something* from her. He came over. 'Why are you frowning, Rosalie?' It was said—deliberately—in a low, almost menacing tone that no one else could hear. Elise was already snatching a last look at her notes before other duties called.

'I'm not frowning, am I?' she answered him lightly.

'Yes you are. At Elise. And me. It's not jealousy, is it?' he growled, half teasing, half truly frustrated.

Her reply was prim. 'Of course it's not!' and he turned impatiently away. He had been impatient and disappointed on Saturday, too. . .

Sitting in a pool of warm sunshine on a picnic rug in a sheltered cove near Boscastle Harbour, after an energetic morning ramble among the craggy ruined walls of Tintagel, they had tried to talk about it, but it hadn't worked.

'What's wrong, Rosalie?' he had said, breaking a silence that had lasted while they ate the salty meal of crumbed plaice and chips. 'Is it the fact that yesterday we so nearly. . .?'

'I—I don't know.'

'Because I can wait for that, you know,' he said gently, then added in a throaty tone, 'Not much longer, mind you. But I'm not waiting just to spring it on you again today, if that's what you're afraid of.'

He had meant the statement to be reassuring, but it hadn't worked that way and he didn't know why. She sat there silently, and he couldn't find words either. He wanted to touch her, hold her as they lay there listening to the waves and the wind, communicate that way, but he had enough sense to master himself. Her body language told him very clearly that this was not what she was asking for.

He felt a helplessness that he was unaccustomed to, and it angered him. Was he wrong? He had begun to feel that this thing between them was so electric, not only physically but emotionally and mentally as well, that it could not go wrong. Now, he was less sure, and he found that this haze of doubt nagged at him and soured his mood.

He had to laugh now, too, at his naïve assumption a few weeks ago that Rosalie would immediately terminate her friendship with Howard Trevalley as a result of his own onslaught on her senses. He had been too confident — no, too arrogant — there, because Rosalie was still seeing the man. And now he caught himself studying Trevalley, trying to see the surgeon as Rosalie saw him. Sometimes it was disturbing. Howard Trevalley had position, status, security, and reliability in demonstrable doses. Were those things important to Rosalie? He didn't know how to find out. . .

Rosalie looked up from her position at the desk in the nurses' station and found that Daniel was still standing there, frowning down at her.

'I've just done Ray Thompson's catheterisation,' he said at once. 'Thought you'd like to hear the result.'

'Yes, I would.'

'No left main artery disease, which is good. Three diseased vessels, though. The left anterior artery is eighty-five per cent blocked, the right anterior artery is eighty per cent, and the circumflex artery about sixty per cent. His heart function is good, however. I think there's a strong case for treating this medically, and since the patient himself is so keen on the approach that's what I'm going to suggest to Trevalley.'

'Howard — er — Mr Trevalley. . .' Both of them noticed the slip and Rosalie flushed. 'Mr Trevalley,'

she said again firmly, 'came to see him this morning,
actually.'

'He did?'

'Yes, and told me privately that after reading the
patient's history, hearing about the persistent chest
pain and seeing the results of the thallium stress test,
he's already pencilled him in for his list tomorrow.'

'No!'

'*Pencilled*,' she stressed, seeing his immediate anger.

'Still, it means an argument, as I half expected. He's
in Cardiac Intensive Care now, and I'm meeting him
down here in a few minutes. . . OK, well, thanks for
warning me. Now I know what I'm up against. . .'

There *was* an argument between Dr Canaday and
Mr Trevalley. They met at Mr Thompson's bedside,
reviewed his case briefly, asked some questions and
then adjourned to a small conference-room opposite
the nurses' station. Fortunately, the glass-panelled
door was nearly sound-proof, but Rosalie still winced
as she caught the faint drumming of raised voices and
saw angry heads shifting back and forth through the
small clear panel.

Daniel needed to be careful. After all, Howard was
senior to him, and that fact was important in the
hospital hierarchy. Then she glimpsed the surgeon's
reddened face and felt a different anxiety. Howard
needed to be careful, too. People began to lose respect
for a doctor who couldn't adapt to new medical
evidence or listen to the arguments of younger
colleagues.

It was several more minutes before they emerged.
Daniel came first. Rosalie didn't see his face, and his
energetic stride as he left the ward could have meant
anger or satisfaction. Howard didn't leave straight
away. He came slowly from the conference-room, and
looked across at the nurses' station to see that Rosalie
was temporarily alone and that she was gazing
worriedly at him.

'Well, I've just had my nose put well out of joint,' he said comfortably, and Rosalie suppressed a sigh of relief. It was going to be all right! At the moment, she didn't have time to wonder whom she had feared for the most. 'Cancel Mr Thompson from your surgical prep list for tomorrow, will you?'

'So you came down on Dr Canaday's side about the bypass?' she ventured.

'I had little choice,' he laughed, 'the number of new American studies on open-heart surgery patients he flung at me! You'd think the whole country had nothing else to do but rush around measuring their heart function and post-operative quality of life. I like that young man!' he finished surprisingly. 'Very much! In fact. . .' he leaned confidentially over the desk after taking a careful glance up and down the corridors to make sure they were still safely alone '. . . I'm hatching out a little plot. Would you like to help me with it?'

'Of course,' Rosalie promised, politely and rashly.

'I think he'd be perfect for my daughter Cathy,' he confided, while Rosalie listened helplessly. 'Someone of his dedication and energy. At the moment she's consumed with this ridiculous notion of going in for general practice in some rural backwater. Wales, no less, is the current favourite. But someone of his ambition. . . He's a good-looking young devil, too — or the junior nurses think so, if I'm any judge of those blushes and giggles of theirs. I'm sure they'd hit it off.'

'H-how old is your daughter?' Rosalie asked haltingly. 'I've forgotten.'

'Twenty-six. Not too late for her to decide on a speciality. Far too soon for her to bury herself in general practice. And he must be thirty-odd. Yes, it's perfect! So, you see. . .' again, his manner became very conspiratorial '. . .I thought I'd organise a brunch. It *is* time you met Cathy. I was sorry about your aunt's invitation last Friday. I—I missed our evening.'

'Yes. . .'

'We must make sure. . . Anyway, are you free for brunch on Sunday? Cathy knows of a very *trendy* place. . .' he brought the word out a little self-consciously '. . .and it's not too far from here. You know Canaday already, and you want to meet Cathy. It'll camouflage the fact that I've got plans for the two of them!'

'It sounds very nice. 'I *would* like to meet Cathy,' Rosalie could only say a little wanly, and Howard Trevalley nodded in satisfaction.

'It's settled, then. I'll pick you up, shall I? Cathy and Canaday can make their own way separately. Say, ten o'clock?'

'I'll look forward to it.'

CHAPTER SIX

IT WAS evening visiting hour on the Kilborne Cardiac Ward, always a busy one on Saturdays. Rosalie didn't mind visiting hour. She always felt that the pleasure of seeing people outweighed how tiring it was for some patients, and she took care that those who were more ill were given quieter rooms.

Beverly Moore seemed to find the visitors more trying, particularly on Saturday evenings. 'Only five more minutes and we can start shuffling them off,' she said. 'Or do you think. . .? Those three with Mr Trelawney in Room 2 seem particularly rowdy. Perhaps they should go now.'

'He's enjoying them immensely,' Rosalie returned placatingly. 'And so is old Mr Stott. He didn't get any visitors today. . .'

'Didn't his daughter come?'

'No, her children are sick—she says. . .and Mr Trelawney's visitors are chatting to Mr Stott as well, which is taking his mind off being lonely.'

'Oh, well, in that case, I suppose. . .'

The five minutes passed quickly and most visitors began to leave without prompting from the nursing staff. Beverly, true to character, began to nudge the reluctant ones along and soon there were only one or two wives or husbands sitting quietly by a bedside and taking the opportunity for private conversation.

Mr Thompson's wife Joan was one of this last handful. Rosalie smiled at her and said hello as she went in to answer Mr Fenstowe's buzzer, which had sounded querulously and lit up a red light on a panel at the nurses' station moments before.

'My feet are cold,' the old man said. 'Come to think of it, I'm cold all over. Can't I have another blanket?'

He said it somewhat indignantly, as if already prepared for his request to be refused. It *wasn't* refused, of course. Rosalie bent down to the bottom drawer in the small chest beside his bed and pulled out a clean blanket of fluffy blue wool. She had to hide a smile. Until today, Mr Fenstowe had been wearing winter flannels, but tonight his wife had brought him a rather gorgeous pair of summer cotton pyjamas with a bright jungle-print pattern, red piping and short legs and sleeves. Very elegant, but no wonder he was cold!

She arranged the blanket over the bed to her patient's satisfaction, a task which seemed to take quite a while, and as she spread and tucked she couldn't help overhearing Mrs Thompson and her husband so close by.

'There's something I've got to tell you love,' the comfortably plump woman was saying. 'Didn't want to say anything while the others were here.'

'Yes?'

'I hope you won't think I did the wrong thing. . .'

'What did you do?'

'I thought about it and thought about it. I decided I wouldn't, then today all of a sudden. . . It's just that he seemed so——'

'*What* did you do, woman?' Mr Thompson burst out, with pardonable impatience.

'I just thought——'

'What did you *do*?'

His face was red now, and as if Mrs Thompson suddenly remembered that he was a cardiac patient and should not be unduly upset she said in a flat voice, 'I had Rufus put down.'

'You *what*?'

'He's seemed so miserable lately, and you know how he smells, and I thought——'

'You mean you've *done* it. It's too late! Rufus is gone! *Joan!*'

He was thunderously angry and deeply anguished at the same time. Even Mr Fenstowe had stopped fussing about his blanket and was staring horrified at his fellow patient. Rosalie was concerned as she saw Mr Thompson's rising colour, and even as she moved across the room to try and calm him it happened.

Anger was replaced by panic and pain on his suffused face and his body contorted as he struggled to sit up higher in bed and find breath. His hand clutched convulsively at his chest in the classic gesture as his heart sent out its signal of agony.

Rosalie waited no longer. She almost flew from the room to the telephone at the nurses' station, and a quick press of a button brought her in touch with Casualty where doctors on call were ready for just this sort of emergency. They would be here on the ward in a matter of minutes.

Meanwhile, there was equipment to be prepared. On Cardiac Intensive Care, all patients were constantly connected to heart-monitoring machines that could be read at a glance from centralised controls at the nurses' station, but here things were less intense. There simply wasn't the equipment or the staff to provide that constant level of observation, and by and large the patients didn't need it. Occasionally, though, like tonight, there was a crisis, and heart-monitoring equipment needed to be rushed to Mr Thompson's bedside. A defibrillator, too, in case the situation grew really serious.

It did. The next half-hour passed with the jumbled rhythm of a nightmare — Mr Thompson's heart had stopped. Daniel Canaday raced on to the ward in the wake of the emergency team from Casualty. . . The green line on the EKG machine remained ominously flat. . . The paddles of the defibrillator were pressed on to the patient's chest and electric current juddered through his body as they attempted to jerk his heart back into life. . . No response. . . Dr Canaday seemed to be pounding Mr Thompson's chest violently with his hands. . . Mrs Thompson was moaning and literally wringing her hands, pressed back against the wall near her husband's bed.

'Again!' came Dr Canaday's urgently barked command. 'And prepare to intubate him! Oxygen. . .'

But before the intubation could be done the line on the echocardiograph lurched with sickening irregularity, stopped, lurched again, and finally, beautifully, settled into the pattern that Rosalie recognised as normal.

Shortly afterwards, the emergency team went away, leaving only Daniel Canaday behind. The patient opened his eyes and stared confusedly at the equipment and at his wife, his face grey. 'What happened?' His voice was very weak. 'I had terrible pain and passed out. Was it. . .?'

'Yes, you had a cardiac infarction,' Daniel said bluntly and wearily. 'It's over now. Your heart rhythm is normal again.'

'But. . . Joan, what were you telling me? You had some news. I've forgotten. . .'

'News?' Daniel asked, turning sharply to the older woman.

'Yes, I——'

'I remember!' Mr Thompson exclaimed, still very weakly. 'Rufus. You had Rufus——'

'Oh, Ray, I'm sorry. I'm so sorry!'

Suddenly Joan Thompson was weeping, the tensions of the past half-hour breaking out like a flood. 'I shouldn't have done it without discussing it with you, but having you in here I've been so worried. I've hardly been sleeping, and then when I got up this morning and found he'd done three dirty messes on the carpet during the night, poor old thing, and his back was getting so red and raw. It was the last straw.

I rang up the vet and he said I could bring him in straight away. He said it was the kindest thing and would be completely painless.'

Rosalie was holding her breath. Sometimes there was a short-term memory loss after an infarction and she had been half hoping that Mr Thompson would not remember the news that appeared to have triggered his heart attack, but in this case it had stayed with him. Daniel was standing there listening to what was going on, clearly impatient, wanting to interrupt and ask questions but Rosalie gave him an imperative glance of warning that told him, Don't say anything yet!

He gave a tiny, curt nod, stepped back a pace and relaxed a little.

Mrs Thompson had finished her emotional outburst now, and she was gazing silently and beseechingly at her husband. For a long time he said nothing. He was still very grey and just seemed to be staring listlessly at the green line on the monitor with its rhythmic pattern and small, regular piping note. Rosalie had a pang of doubt. Had she been right to let the couple talk this through? Or was it too soon and too stressful?

'You did the right thing, love,' Mr Thompson said at last, answering Rosalie's question as well as his wife's. His breathing was laboured and his words clearly came with an effort but his colour was beginning to return to normal. 'I wish. . . It would have been nice if you'd waited to talk to me about it, but. . . I understand why you didn't.'

'It was just the last straw this morning.'

'I know. I'd probably have felt the same if I were you. And I said a decent goodbye to him before I came in here.'

They kept on talking about the beloved old dog, Mrs Thompson prompting her husband's memories of the animal in his heyday, while he nodded tiredly and let a pale smile wander over his face every now and then.

Daniel drew Rosalie aside. 'The news about the dog triggered the attack?'

'I'd say so. He was very angry and upset.'

'I think you were right to let them talk it through. Even though he's very tired it's obviously on his mind. Better to resolve it now so he can have a good night.'

'Yes, I thought so,' Rosalie nodded. 'You'll send him up to CICU, I suppose?'

'Actually, not tonight. They've only got one bed left up there. If it's all right with you. . . If things are quiet enough in here. . .'

'So far,' Rosalie nodded. 'Of course it's the night staff who'll bear the brunt of the extra work after we go off at eleven. Perhaps I could stay. . .'

'What, and be too tired for Howard's brunch tomorrow?'

'Oh! Well, yes, there is that,' she answered a little lamely, not sure how to interpret his tone. Neither of them had referred to tomorrow's social event until now. Rosalie hadn't even known if he knew who would be in the party, but it seemed that he did.

'I'm looking forward to meeting Cathy Trevalley,' he said. 'Aren't you?'

'Oh. . .yes.'

'In any case, there shouldn't be any further problem with Mr Thompson tonight if my analysis is correct. That infarct must have been caused by arterial spasm. Trevalley will be. . .not pleased, I suppose, but. . .'

'What do you mean?'

'There'll have to be a bypass now. We can't risk another attack like that. Theoretically, his arteries are clear enough, but if they spasm in that way. . . No, it has to be surgery.' He shook his head, defeat evident in the tired fall of his usually so dynamic features. Impulsively, Rosalie reached out and touched his arm.

'You're blaming yourself, aren't you?'

'Of course.'

'And yet —'

'I know. It's an emotional response, not a logical one.'

Gently, he removed her hand from his forearm and she felt a little rejected by the gesture. His moment of weakness and doubt had passed now, it seemed, and his detailed instructions about nursing care for Mr Thompson were made briskly and efficiently. A few minutes later he had left the ward.

Mr Thompson remained hooked up to monitoring equipment for the rest of the night and his wife remained at his bedside, but there was no further drama. Rosalie was able to leave promptly at eleven after giving a thorough rundown to the incoming night staff, and when she woke in the morning she made a quick call to the ward and found that her patient's condition was still stable and satisfactory.

Putting down the phone after her short conversation with Louise Porter, however, she found that she was feeling rather restless and dissatisfied. She hadn't slept particularly well, and after waking at half-past six she had lain in bed for another useless half-hour, unable to get back to sleep. It was now only just after seven, and Howard wasn't calling for her until ten.

I'll go into the garden! she decided.

Rosalie had neglected her rambling territory shamefully of late, and she was well aware that Daniel Canaday was the reason. Too many hours that could have been pleasurably spent among seedlings and flowers had instead been squandered on restless wandering along the cliff path or idle lolling on a garden seat in the sun. This past week, though, she had forced herself to tackle the rapidly burgeoning weeds. It had been a chore, not a pleasure, because she had only done it out of a fierce need to prove to herself that life would continue quite normally once this brief flaring thing with Daniel was ended.

Yes, it was pointless to think of it in any other way. Last weekend's tension and awkwardness had shown her the inevitability of an ending and now she was waiting for it — and almost wanting it — to come. Once it did, then she would be able to get on with life again. Meanwhile, there was this awkward brunch to get through. . .

Howard arrived promptly at ten, and she was ready, dressed in a warm-toned floral skirt and a Swiss cotton blouse of soft apricot. Howard seemed keyed up as they drove.

'I've never tried anything like this before,' he said as they wound through the village, narrowly missing an indignant terrier defending its boundaries.

'Brunch?' queried Rosalie absently. She was busy wondering whether Daniel was looking forward to today, and thinking back on his deceptively bland remark about Cathy Trevalley yesterday.

'No!' The surgeon gave a hoot of laughter. 'Matchmaking!'

'Oh. . .'

'It's more of a woman's game, after all.' He said it as if realising suddenly that such machinations were somewhat beneath him. 'Perhaps I'd better leave it to you.'

'Leave what, exactly?' She was irritated at his attitude.

'Oh, you know. . .the little ways women have to smooth things out between people. You must be sure to say something to Canaday. . .something about his work, what a fine doctor he is.'

'Must I?' Her irritation was growing.

'Yes. . . At least,' he sighed, 'I hope this brunch was a good idea. You know, since Helen died I've found this sort of thing so hard — knowing how to talk to Cathy, how to find out if she is happy — all these dealings between people. Helen was so good at all that.'

He lapsed into silence and Rosalie found that her irritation had evaporated, to be replaced by a warm, sympathetic sort of feeling. Poor Howard! He had been married to Helen for nearly thirty years, and like many men of his generation he had left social and personal matters largely in his wife's tactful hands. Could he be blamed now if he was sometimes awkward in dealing with new relationships?

Not for the first time, Rosalie found that when she rationalised his behaviour she could forgive it, and she resolved to make things as smooth as possible for him this morning. She would be attentive to his every word and need, and would be as warm and friendly as she could to Cathy, even if she detested the girl on sight. As for Daniel, he could take care of himself. . .

Indeed he could! He was already waiting for them at the restaurant and had commandeered the perfect table in a delightful courtyard at the back. In a sheltered corner, the chairs received the ideal amount of dappled shade from an overhanging wattle tree, while the white tablecloth glowed brilliantly in a shaft of sunlight. Cathy had already arrived as well, and the two of them stood smilingly as they waited for Howard and Rosalie to approach the table.

'Goodness! Are we late or are you two early?' Howard laughed a little forcedly as Daniel held a chair back for Rosalie.

'A little late, I think,' Rosalie put in gently. 'My fault,' she explained to the two younger people. 'I had to let the cat out at home, then I got a stone in my shoe as we came along the street.'

Howard made introductions — unnecessarily in the case of Cathy and Daniel as they seemed to have struck up an amicable acquaintance already — and everyone sat down. Menus were soon brought, and Rosalie studied the appetising descriptions hungrily. Two hours in the garden this morning on an empty stomach had given her quite an appetite. That smoked

salmon platter, with herb rolls, brioche, salad, fruit
and cream cheese sounded delicious.

'Ready to order, sir?' The supercilious young waiter
took the senior surgeon by surprise, appearing silently
behind his left shoulder. 'Oh — er —' Howard turned
awkwardly, craning his neck stiffly to look at him. 'I'll
have the eggs Benedict, with coffee and orange juice.
And the others, ah. . .'

'The cheese and salad platter, please,' Cathy said,
'And a glass of chablis.'

'I'll have the salmon and salad platter,' Daniel came
in. 'And some chablis as well. That sounds lovely,
Cathy.'

He grinned with a nuance of wicked complicity that
Rosalie did not miss. Cathy grinned back. Blonde,
with a frank dappling of freckles on nose and cheeks,
she was not quite what Rosalie had been expecting —
although when Rosalie thought about it she found that
she did not know what mental image she *had* formed
of Howard Trevalley's daughter before this meeting.

'Oh. . .' Howard was saying a little uncertainly.
'You two are treating this as lunch, are you?'

'I'll have the eggs Benedict as well, thank you,'
Rosalie put in quickly, turning to the waiter. 'And
coffee and orange juice.'

Out of the corner of her eye, she saw that Howard
seemed relieved at her choice. She hadn't wanted eggs
Benedict at all, and, like the other two, had been
much more ready for the cool, clean tastes of a salad,
but conforming to Howard's choice brought her the
reward of seeing him relax, so she decided it was worth
it.

'I haven't had eggs Benedict for years,' the surgeon
confessed, with a disarmingly boyish smile, and
Rosalie agreed.

'Yes, my mouth's watering at the very thought.'

Somehow, the fact that their menu choices had
fallen into pairs set the tone for the rest of the meal.

Daniel started asking Cathy a series of questions about her career plans, while Rosalie and Howard listened like indulgent but slightly bemused parents.

'I want to be in a practice where I can follow my patients through from chickenpox to childbirth,' Cathy explained earnestly to Daniel, and he nodded intently. 'It's old-fashioned,' the young doctor admitted. 'I want to make house calls!'

'Perhaps it's not old-fashioned at all,' the cardiologist teased. 'Perhaps you're in the vanguard of a return to some of the tried and true values of medicine. Getting back to treating each patient like a whole animal instead of like a machine, where the broken bits can be replaced one at a time.'

'It's interesting that you should compare it to animals,' Cathy said, 'because I sometimes think that vets treat their patients more *humanly*, more like feeling, sentient creatures than doctors do these days. At least, that's how it is with the vet—um—vets that I know. . .'

'You've never said all this to me, Catherine,' Howard put in rather too heartily.

'You never give me a chance, Dad,' she answered cheekily, with a disarming grin.

'Don't I?'

'No!'

'Oh, well. . . I suppose I feel. . .' He trailed off uncertainly, and once again Rosalie, who had been sitting silently, came to the rescue.

'Your feelings about your future are fairly, new, though, aren't they, Cathy?' she asked in a friendly way. 'Perhaps this is the first time you've put it into words to anyone.'

'Actually, yes. Daniel managed to ask the right questions, I suppose.' She smiled at the cardiologist again and Rosalie saw that Howard was very pleased at how the two of them were getting on. In fact, he nudged Rosalie's knee with his under the table, a private gesture that was clearly meant to say, It's working!

The four meals arrived and Rosalie ate hers woodenly, fighting against a despondency which she told herself was ridiculous. It was a glorious morning, and the fragrant clematis that crawled over the stone walls of this courtyard was sweetening the air with a delightful, ineffably subtle perfume. The eggs Benedict, after all, were delicious, even if she did still have a yen for those crisp salads on Cathy's and Daniel's plates. Conversation was flowing freely. So what was wrong?

I feel old, she realised. I've been paired with Howard today, and I feel in my fifties, while Daniel and Cathy are young. Oh! This is idiotic! It's not as if he's flirting with her! And if he is. . .yes, he *is* a bit! she decided suddenly and contrarily. . .he has a perfect right to. I'm here with Howard. Cathy is charming. They look good together. . .

As if aware of this himself, the cardiologist continued to draw out the young would-be general practitioner.

'I *have* to live where I can ride!' she was saying. 'And I have to have *time* to ride. During those toughest few years of training when I barely got on a horse from one month to the next I nearly went crazy. Ninety hours a week stuck in the depths of a hospital. . . That's not for me!'

'Oh, now, Cathy!' Howard protested. 'Do I work ninety hours a week? Do you, Daniel?'

'Actually, about seventy at the moment, sometimes more,' the cardiologist said quietly.

'No, Dad, but *I'd* have to,' Cathy answered seriously. 'For several years, anyway, until I was fully qualified. I'm bright,' she conceded easily, 'but I'm not brilliant, and you need to be, these days, to specialise successfully. I just don't have it in me. I don't have the *will*.'

'Then you're making the right decision,' Daniel

nodded. 'Sorry, sir. . .' He grinned unrepentantly at the senior surgeon. 'I'm not saying the right thing, am I?'

'No problem, no problem,' Howard replied, surprisingly relaxed.

He really does hope they'll fall in love, Rosalie realised. That's more important to him already than the idea of Cathy specialising.

'You've managed to get Cathy to explain her feelings more cogently in one morning than I have in a lifetime,' Howard went on. 'It's the generation gap, I suppose.' He smiled at Rosalie, making her his ally in seniority.

'Watch your coffee!' Rosalie put in quickly, as his wrist, clad in a clean white shirt-sleeve, came dangerously close to toppling the refilled cup.

'Oops! Thanks.'

He drew back and moved the cup out of harm's way, while Rosalie heard her own words echoing in her head. It was such a staid, wifely thing to say. . .

Knowing it was unfair, she felt angry with Daniel. Need he fall in so enthusiastically with Howard's plans? It was almost as if the senior surgeon had actually *asked* him to consider Cathy as a future lover. He was positively flirting with her now, and she seemed to be enjoying it. It would hardly be surprising if a genuine attraction developed between them.

Brunch was over at last. 'I must take Rosalie home,' Howard announced, then added hopefully. 'But Trefusis Park is very near here if you two feel like a walk.'

His daughter and Daniel made non-committal responses, and ambiguous goodbyes were said. Rosalie and Howard drove away, not knowing whether Daniel and Cathy would spend the rest of the morning together or not.

'It went well, I think,' the surgeon said as soon as he was alone with Rosalie in the car.

'Yes. . .although Cathy seems pretty certain of her plans about general practice.'

'Oh, she's brighter than she gives herself credit for,' Howard explained seriously. 'With someone like Canaday to help and encourage her, she'd easily get through cardiology.'

'Which is it you want most?' Rosalie asked with a laugh that was meant to be light, although it sounded very forced to her own ears. 'A daughter who's a cardiologist. . .or a son-in-law?'

He gave a shout of laughter. 'Both!'

When they got to the cottage, Rosalie wondered whether she should ask him in. The invitation hovered on the tip of her tongue, but in the end she simply said, 'That was a lovely idea to go out for brunch. Thank you, Howard. I enjoyed it very much.'

Alone in the house five minutes later, she almost regretted her reluctance. The cottage was too quiet, suddenly, and the rest of the day stretched ahead. There was more to be done in the garden, of course, as well as a dozen tiny tasks in the house — mending a fallen hem, cleaning the refrigerator, writing cards and letters to friends. None of these activities appealed, and once again the cliff-top path beckoned to her restless spirit. Impulsively, she gave in to the need to breathe sea air and hurried upstairs to change into some comfortably baggy washed denim shorts and a matching blouse, teamed with white jogging shoes.

She set off at a brisk pace, swinging a straw hat carelessly by its blue ribbon ties and letting the drumming rhythm of her feet on the hard clay of the path drown all thoughts. In the shelter of the rolling hills, the sun kissed her skin hotly and the summer grasses gave off a warm, fragrant scent. Up on the cliffs, the breeze was tangy and refreshing, cool but not cold.

I hope I'm never too old to do this, she was thinking, when suddenly there came the thud of footsteps behind her and a hand reached out to grab her shoulder.

With a gasp of fear, she whirled around. . .and it was Daniel.

'My God, you can walk fast!' he said. 'I've been panting after you like a spent fox for the last ten minutes!'

He wasn't panting, of course. He was grinning, and tendrils of black hair, slightly too long, whipped around his neck. With her breath caught in her throat and her legs drained of their strength, Rosalie couldn't find a reply. Absently she tied the straw hat on her head but Daniel stepped forward and pulled it loose again, so that he could run his fingers briefly and wordlessly through her wind-blown tresses, before touching a short, searing kiss to her lips.

'I felt like a spy,' he said, 'skulking around to make sure Howard had gone. I didn't dare drive down your street at first, then from a distance I saw you up here and I saw you were alone so I parked and ran, and here I am.'

'Why did you come?' she asked lightly, not daring to let him see how happy she was.

'To scold you, actually.'

'*Scold* me?'

'Yes, for playing up to Howard like that this morning.'

'*I* was playing up!' She was indignant. 'What about you and Cathy?'

He looked sheepish. 'Cathy's nice. I like her. She needs someone on her side against that father of hers.' His tone allied Rosalie with Howard, as they had been allied this morning. But Daniel saw the way her face had closed and hardened. 'Hey! What's wrong?'

'Nothing.' It seemed too petty to talk about her feelings. Brought out into the open by clumsy words, this morning's doubt would sound ridiculous.

'Nothing,' he echoed patiently. 'OK.'

And he didn't pursue the subject any further. At the time it didn't seem to matter. He grabbed her hand

and pulled her along the cliff path, and they spent an hour energetically exploring the scalloped coves and headlands like children before turning back, tired and wind-swept and hungry to the cottage.

'Are you asking me in for a snack?' he said shamelessly when they were within sight of the house. She could see his white car parked outside her front gate and was glad that Howard was not given to dropping in on impulse.

'If you're hungry,' she answered.

They went inside and Rosalie realised that her windswept hair was a tangled mess. Needing to tidy it before she thought about food, she hurried upstairs and stood in front of the mirror, brushing the red strands with light strokes as she wondered a little bemusedly whether it was only the wind that had given her cheeks such colour and her eyes such a sparkle.

Then she heard a movement behind her, whirled around and found that he was leaning in the open doorway, studying her even more closely than she had been studying her reflection. He smiled as he saw her startled reaction and didn't tear his hungry eyes away. Surprised and made vulnerable by him for the second time that day, Rosalie was angry, seethingly angry all of a sudden.

'What are you doing, Daniel?'

'Looking at you.'

'I can see that. *Why* are you looking at me?'

'Isn't it obvious?'

'For heaven's sake!' She was trembling and her voice was low and throaty with a rage that she didn't even try to understand or control. 'You were flirting blatantly with Cathy three hours ago. I felt as if you'd almost consigned me to the role of your stepmother. Now you expect me to ——'

'Just a minute, Rosalie! I'm not "expecting" anything. What did *you* "expect" this morning? That we should have behaved as we normally do when we're

together? Like this?' He was close to her now, his
hands hovering around her and his breathing fanning
the tumbling mane of her hair although he did not
touch her. 'Hardly able to keep our hands off each
other?' It was a low, sensuous growl, nakedly explicit
about the physical attraction they each felt. 'Hanging
on each other's every word, scarcely bothering to finish
our sentences half the time because ——'

'No, but ——'

'What is this really about? Lately you've been ——'

'Lately I've been realistic,' she came in with a blunt,
hard edge to her voice.

'Realistic? What's that supposed to mean?'

There was a long moment of silence in which both
held themselves warily, still fighting the magnetism
that pulled them powerfully towards each other.

'It means,' she said at last on a careful breath, 'that
I think the time has come for this to end. I've tried to
. . .to look ahead. . .and I can't see that anything can
come of this but awkwardness. . .and possibly pain.
Whether it's next week or next month or ——' She
stopped.

Until she made the stumbling speech, she hadn't
known that this was what she intended to say. It was
an expression of all the doubts she had felt all along,
an emotional outburst that was begging to be
contradicted.

Yes, she wanted him to take her in his arms, kiss
her, speak hotly against her mouth, deny everything
she had said, tell her that it wasn't true, she was
wrong, she was wrong about it all because he loved
her and they would find a way to make it work.

But he said none of this, and he didn't make any
attempt to touch her. Instead, his words were controlled and simple. 'All right. Yes. There have been
problems. It seems you've been thinking about them
more than I have. I didn't think you'd be so afraid

of —— But all right. I guess there's nothing more to be said, then.'

'No, I don't think so. Perhaps you'd better ——'

'Leave?' He quirked an eyebrow sardonically. 'I'd hardly stay, in the circumstances, would I?'

'I suppose not,' she murmured, feeling the comment like a slap in the face.

Awkward silence hung in the air as he turned and left the room. With her freshly brushed hair floating like a rich cloud around her face Rosalie followed him down the stairs, a lifetime of good manners dictating that she should see him out, even in these painful circumstances. He saw her behind him only as she held the door after he had passed through it. He was turning back to close it, and his movement towards the handle, although checked abruptly, brought them within inches of each other once again.

He pulled back with a hiss of breath and she knew exactly why. Even now, their physical effect on each other was electric. Tiredly, she acknowledged to herself that this had been much of the problem all along.

CHAPTER SEVEN

'Now, Sister Crane, Staff Nurse Moore, and—er—
juniors, I'd like you to meet my daughter, Dr Cathy
Trevalley.'

Rosalie suppressed a smile at the pride which
vibrated in Howard's tone as he said his daughter's
name, with that distinguished word 'doctor' at the
beginning of it. She also suppressed irritation. Cathy
had smiled and said covertly to her a minute ago,
'Sorry if I'm not very friendly. Dad tells me you and I
are not supposed to know each other socially already!'

It was so typical of Howard that Rosalie had nodded
easily and betrayed no surprise. Cathy had made a
small grimace that said, Dad has these funny ideas!
but Rosalie hadn't felt at home enough yet with the
younger woman to return it. Besides, it seemed a little
disloyal to Howard, and she ought not to be disloyal
to the senior surgeon. . .when she had made up her
mind to marry him if he asked her.

Only a week had passed since the painful rupture
with Daniel Canaday, but it had been a very long
week. Sleepless, too. Each night Rosalie lay in bed
wondering whether she had done the right thing, and
each night she drifted into a tense, unrestful slumber
deciding that she had. The time had come to do what
she should have been doing all along—building a safe,
unexciting but utterly suitable relationship with a man
who *didn't* turn her inside out and upside-down every
time they met.

That weekend away with Howard that had been
bandied about half-heartedly for weeks—she ought to
drop some brazen hints about it, or, better, adopt
some of Daniel's own frankness in dealing with the

issue. She ought to name a date and make Howard pencil it in his diary! And she ought to refuse to go along with the surgeon's coy pretence that he and she had no relationship outside the world of the hospital.

Now was not the moment to rebel, however. 'Pleased to meet you,' she said conventionally to Cathy, and Howard hid his discomfiture behind a fussy cough.

'My daughter is interested in cardiac care,' he said, ignoring Cathy's glare of denial. 'She's taking a break before starting a locum position in general practice in Wales, and I've arranged for her to spend several days here at the hospital. She'll spend most of her time with me, of course, but she'll also be tagging along with Dr Canaday while he shows her the ropes from a cardiologist's point of view. I'm sure I don't need to ask you to accommodate her in every way. Now, Cathy. . .'

He led her away from the small group of nurses gathered at the central nurses' station and gave her a private tour of the ward. Rosalie went on with her work, giving an appearance of calm that was somewhat deceptive. This was the last thing she needed now — to see Howard attempting — and very possibly succeeding — to further the friendship between his daughter and Daniel Canaday.

The cardiologist arrived while she was still struggling to make sense of the paperwork in front of her.

'I've given the OK for Ray Thompson to come back down here,' he said to Rosalie, leaning over the desk and dispensing with any greeting. 'He's doing very well after the bypass last week. You have an appropriate bed, do you?'

'Only one, actually, but yes,' she nodded. 'It's back where he was before, which I think he'll be pleased about.'

'Will he be pleased about hearing old Mr Fenstowe's complaints?' the cardiologist queried teasingly.

'Mr Fenstowe was discharged yesterday,' Rosalie reminded him.

'That's right,' Daniel frowned. Then, 'Is Mr Trevalley here with his daughter?'

'Yes.' So Daniel was pretending now, too!

'Good.'

'I think they're ——'

'I'll find them.'

Having shaken off her assistance, he was gone and a moment later she heard his cheerful greeting along the corridor. 'Cathy! Enjoying it so far? It's a good idea for you to spend some time here, I think, because. . .' Then his voice faded. Evidently the two of them had turned into a side-room together, as Howard appeared shortly afterwards on his own.

'Well, that's all set up,' he said, very satisfied.

Rosalie glanced around and found that the two of them were alone for the moment. 'Is our Friday night thing happening this week?' she asked. It was the first time she had brought up the subject herself. In the past, Howard had always been the one to issue the invitation.

'Yes. Oh, yes!' he answered, clearly taken by surprise. 'If you'd like to. Of course.'

'The usual time?'

'Certainly.'

'And perhaps we could try somewhere new this week. I think we've tried everything at Baldwin's!'

'I suppose we have,' he laughed thinly. 'Yes, that's true. I like familiar food, you see. But Cathy teases me about it. I should show her that I'm keeping up with. . .what is it?. . .*nouvelle cuisine*?'

'Then let's find somewhere that does *nouvelle cuisine*,' she agreed, and they left it at that.

Cathy Trevalley's presence at the hospital was accepted quickly by everyone. She was a frank, friendly young woman who had more than enough sense not to step on anyone's toes professionally, and a winning bedside manner that meant almost every patient accepted yet another intrusive human presence poking and prodding them physically and verbally. If Howard thought that the stint of working with cardiac patients was turning Cathy's thoughts towards specialising in the field, though, he was very much mistaken, Rosalie concluded.

Clues to this mounted daily. On Wednesday, the phone rang and it was Howard himself ringing down from CICU. 'Where's Cathy? I've been expecting her up here for the past ten minutes!'

'She's here,' Rosalie promised. 'I'll go and find her.'

'If you would.'

She poked her head in at each door and finally found Cathy in one of the four-bed rooms standing beside John Powys's bed. The middle-aged Welshman looked happy and animated. 'Now, my place, it used to be down the valley a bit from Llandovery. But your friend, tell me again?'

'He's a vet,' Cathy said. 'He has a practice in Llandilo.'

'My sister lives in Llandilo——!'

'Dr Trevalley. . .' Rosalie interrupted tentatively.

'Oh, yes, sorry, are you waiting for me?' Cathy turned guiltily. 'I've just found out that Mr Powys, here, is from quite near Llandilo—er—Llandovery . . .where I'll be going for this locum position.'

'Lovely!' Rosalie replied appropriately, wondering why Cathy's cheeks were so becomingly flushed beneath the dappling of freckles. 'But your father just phoned down from Cardiac Intensive Care, and. . .'

'Oh, heavens!' The young doctor looked at her watch even more guiltily. 'I'm supposed to be up there! I must fly! But Mr Powys. . .' she turned to the older man '. . .don't you dare get yourself discharged without telling me more about Llandovery!'

'Oh, I won't! I won't!' he laughed comfortably,

looking more cheerful than he had for days. Rosalie knew that there was no danger of his being discharged. He had a rare heart complaint and, after much testing and discussion, his team of doctors—including Daniel and Peter Myers—had decided on a transplant as soon as a donor became available. Mr Powys had consented to the plan but had been depressed by it. For the moment, though, under Cathy Trevalley's influence, he seemed to have forgotten all about it.

She *will* make a good general practitioner, Rosalie found herself thinking, as if the matter was a foregone conclusion.

On Thursday, there was further evidence of this.

'That was the admin office,' Margaret Binns reported, after replacing the telephone receiver at about seven-thirty in the morning.

'Oh, yes?' said Rosalie, a little absently. Their shift had only just started, and, as was becoming a pattern, she hadn't slept well last night.

'Leonard Robinson is being admitted again. It's only about four weeks since he was discharged, isn't it?'

'I think so.' She struggled to remember the details of the businessman's case, and quickly it came back to her.

'That's right. Admitted to Casualty complaining of intense chest pain, he was found to have had a heart attack and was brought here to the coronary care unit. The pain ebbed after a day and it was decided that his heart attack had been uncomplicated and that further problems would be treated medicinally.'

He had been discharged after about ten days with nitroglycerine and beta blockers presribed as medication, and the ward staff had given him little further thought. He had been a pleasant enough patient, a little
testy at times, but new patients had taken his place and his home life had apparently been stable, giving no cause for ongoing concern. In short, he was one of

the ward's many patients that left no lasting impression. You simply couldn't remember everyone!

Now he was back. 'Another heart attack?' Rosalie asked.

'Don't know,' answered Margaret.

The phone rang again and this time it was Daniel Canaday. Why didn't I let Margaret pick it up again? Rosalie asked herself uselessly.

'Has Mr Robinson arrived up with you yet?'

'No,' she said. 'We've just heard he's being admitted. Was it another heart attack?'

'Not indicated by the EKG. I took a look at him down in Casualty about half an hour ago, but didn't get much of a chance to talk, so let me know when he's settled in and I'll come up. Meanwhile, could you ring his GP and tell him what's happened?'

'Of course.'

'Thanks. Bye.'

He rang off, as busy and impersonal as a cardiologist could be. Gritting her teeth and blocking off all painful thoughts, Rosalie reached for the phone once again. She needed to call Patient Records and get Leonard Robinson's file sent up in order to find out the name of his GP. That information should have been on the file card kept up here on the ward for some time after each patient's discharge, but for some reason it hadn't been recorded.

The patient arrived on the ward before his file did, and he was soon settled into a suitable bed, but Rosalie hesitated about ringing Dr Canaday again just yet. Mr Robinson was both anxious and annoyed, nervous about missing work and angry with his wife who had left the hospital while he was still being examined in Casualty and now could not be reached on the phone at home.

'Where on earth *is* she?' the irate patient exclaimed, insisting on remaining by the phone until he had succeeded in tracking her down, and demanding that a bedside telephone be connected immediately.

'His file's here,' reported a slightly vague third-year, Mary Clark, and Rosalie turned to it gratefully, finding the name of his general practitioner without difficulty. Brian Eltham. She got on to him at once and told him the news.

'Oh, dear!' was his response.

'His cardiologist here, Dr Canaday, would like to speak to you about his case. Can he ring you back? He should be here in a few minutes.'

'Hmm. . . I have a number of patients this morning, due to start coming at any minute,' he answered. He sounded like an older man, and seemed reluctant at the possibility of having his morning schedule run late. Perhaps he had golf this afternoon. 'Isn't there another doctor I can talk to now?'

'I'll see,' Rosalie promised, then, putting her hand on the phone, she told Mary Clark, 'Have Dr Canaday paged straight away, could you? We'll see how soon we can get him up here. He could ring Dr Eltham from Casualty, or wherever he is now, but I'm sure he'll want to have Mr Robinson's notes in front of him.'

She smiled abstractedly at Cathy Trevalley, who had just arrived on the ward, and was about to turn back to the phone when the pretty doctor said, 'Is it something I could help with?'

Rosalie hesitated, then said, 'Actually, yes.' She made sure that the receiver was well sound-proofed by her hand then added, 'Keep Dr Eltham talking, would you? He wants to talk to Dr Canaday and Dr Canaday wants to talk to him but they're both busy — or claim to be! — and I know if they miss each other by two minutes and then can't get in touch for the rest of the morning they'll be irritated and they'll probably blame *me*!'

She knew by now that it was the kind of thing you

could safely say to Cathy Trevalley and be sure of a comradely laugh, and she was right. Cathy took the phone quickly, stretched its cord over to the quietest corner of the nurses' station and was soon involved in an intense discussion with the GP on the other end of the line.

Meanwhile, Rosalie left to answer an urgent and anxious summons from a junior and when she returned to the nurses' station several minutes later with the minor problem satisfactorily resolved she heard Mary Clark's report. 'Still no response from Dr Canaday. Shall I have him paged again?'

'No, he'll ring when he can, or he'll just turn up,' Rosalie prophesied—accurately, as it turned out two minutes later, when he strode on to the ward. Rosalie pointed to the phone and said, 'Mr Robinson's GP— Dr Eltham,' then she looked around for the file and found that Dr Trevalley had it. Dr Trevalley was also waving Daniel away, refusing to hand over the phone. Soon, however, she wound up her conversation with the GP in a friendly way and gave Daniel the receiver with a smile.

Then she turned to Rosalie. 'I haven't left Daniel much to find out,' she said.

'Dr Eltham was helpful and useful, then?'

'Oh, yes! We had a good talk. I found out that his marriage is breaking up and his business is in trouble.'

'Dr *Eltham's*?'

'No. Sorry. Pronoun ambiguity. Mr *Robinson's*.'

Daniel had already put down the phone. 'Dr Eltham says he's filled you in,' he said to Cathy with a touch of accusation in his tone, and Rosalie wondered if she had done the right thing. She had intended that Cathy should simply keep the conversational ball in the air till Daniel arrived to do the real work, but she might have known that young Dr Trevalley would immediately strike up a rapport with a fellow GP and would find out all the relevant human details of the patient's life.

'Sorry,' the freckled blonde was grinning now. 'I told him I was sure he had a better insight into the underlying emotional factors in Mr Robinson's life than any specialist ever could and he got the bit between his teeth and told me everything.'

'Hmm, well you overstepped your boundaries a little,' Daniel said, then conceded, 'But I'll let it pass this time.'

'Don't worry,' she promised, slightly repentant now. 'Today's my last day.'

'Is it?' He seemed interested, surprised. . .and disappointed, or so Rosalie's less than *disinterested* eyes and ears told her. 'I thought it was another two weeks before you started in Llandovery.'

'It is,' Cathy acknowledged, then added, sounding a little flustered, 'But I thought. . .you know. . .it'd be nice to get settled into the cottage I've rented, get to know the district. . .and that sort of thing.'

'Right,' he nodded, studying her with slightly narrowed eyes.

There was an undercurrent to the exchange that Rosalie didn't understand, and she was distracted from the discussion that followed between the two of them about Mr Robinson. Did Daniel have the same struggle to remain professional that she was having since they had agreed not to see each other? she wondered.

As he stood with Cathy discussing the details of Leonard Robinson's case, Rosalie found it almost impossible to tear her eyes away from those soft curls of his around his ears and neck, the dent in his upper lip and the tiny white scar on his jawline. . .and that opening in his shirt-front where his tanned collarbone just began to show. Even the way he nodded his head — such a direct, assured, thoughtful movement — had the power to set her emotions in turmoil.

Perhaps if I could be friends with him. . . I may *have* to be friends with him. If he and Cathy should get seriously involved, if they married. . .and if I marry Howard I'll be his mother-in-law! No, *step-mother*-in-law. That sounds even worse!

Cathy left a few minutes later, and Rosalie turned to Daniel, with a carefully summoned smile. 'Did she put your nose out of joint, then, finding out so much important background from Dr Eltham?'

'What?' He gazed at her blankly, his black eyes scarcely seeing her at all, then his face cleared. 'No, not at all!' Now he seemed irritated at her flippant suggestion. 'What a ridiculous idea! In fact, I'm grateful for her help and for the information. She'll make an excellent general practitioner. And now I must go and see Mr Robinson!'

He strode away without another word and Rosalie felt as one of her beloved rose bushes must have felt when it put out its buds too soon and had them seared away by a late, unexpected frost. She was still raw from the exchange three and a half hours later at lunchtime when she sat by herself with a tray in front of her, glad that there were no friends here today to beckon her to their table.

But then she looked up and saw Daniel threading his way between the tables with a tray of his own. He wasn't making for her table, but for one some yards away, in a direct line between the long serving counter and the place where she sat, so it was only an unlucky chance that made their eyes meet. And at that moment the table he had chosen was grabbed and filled by four enthusiastic medical students, flinging bags and books on its laminated surface before going to join the queue for food.

Daniel hesitated, slopping coffee from a brimming cup on to its saucer below, and Rosalie swallowed her reluctance. It would be very unnatural and awkward if they never spoke to each other!

'There's room here,' she told him, beckoning and raising her voice slightly as the cafeteria was becoming crowded and noisy.

He stared at her, his hesitation very apparent, but finally came over and put his tray down on the table in front of a spare seat.

'That new group of students seem like a particularly exuberant lot,' she said, too brightly. 'A beefy bunch, too. I hope they all go into orthopaedics, where all that muscle can be put to good use. Even the women seem——'

'Rosalie, stop!' he cut in abruptly, his voice low and vibrant. She was shocked into silence and could only stare at him across the trays of food that both remained untouched. 'Is this what you expect of our relationship from now on? That it should turn into a chatty sort of friendship?'

'I was hoping——'

'Because you must see that it's impossible.' He suppressed an oath.

'Why?' she returned, her own anger mounting in response to his. 'Surely it would be civilised to at least try and pretend that——'

'Civilised! I don't give a straw about being *civilised*.' He said the word with bitter derision. 'I'm not a particularly civilised person when it comes to certain areas of my life, Rosalie. If you want things to be civil—and social—and sensible—then you'd better choose——' He broke off abruptly. 'I guess you *have* chosen him. It's Howard, isn't it? I've lost out to Howard Trevalley.' There was a cruel amusement in his tone now.

'No. . .' But her denial was weak and it received only a cynically raised eyebrow in response.

The tiny gesture made her angry again and she easily could have burst out to him that she didn't want Howard at all, she wanted *him*, only that wouldn't work because at this point in her life she was 'civil—

and social — and sensible' enough to want more than
just the heady fulfilment of her body's needs. And if
Daniel couldn't offer more, then she would build a
relationship with someone who could!

But Daniel didn't give her the chance to speak. 'So
is it understood between us, Rosalie?' The way he said
her name still made her feel as if his hands were
caressing her. 'We'll be as friendly as we need to be
on the ward, but anywhere else. . .can we cut the
pretence? We've burned each other, and I, at least,
can't stand to go on chafing at the wounds.'

'I thought we might organise another foursome this
weekend,' Howard said to Rosalie as they chatted over
coffee at the end of a pleasant evening out.

'That sounds nice!' He didn't seem to notice the
forced quality of her reply, fortunately.

'Very casual,' he amplified now. 'I realised you've
never been to my place.'

'No, that's true. . .' Her spirits lifted a little,
although she didn't fully analyse why. Indeed, she
would have been shocked to realise that at some
subconscious level she was thinking, If I love his house,
then it'll be easier to think of spending my life with
him.

'So I thought, if you're free, Sunday afternoon.
Lunch and a bit of a ramble around the place. It's
Cathy's last weekend with me before she goes off into
the wilds of Wales, and I've already checked that
Canaday's available. We might send them off on
horseback together and have some time to ourselves.'

'Oh, good.' There was a small silence, then she
ventured to point out, 'But will it do much good trying
to bring them together like this when she'll be so far
away?'

'Wales isn't that far! And he's the kind of fellow
who doesn't mind a mad dash in the car every week-

end. Men have boundless energy at that age, the scoundrels!'

'I gather *you* did!' she teased, not without effort.

'Well, it was different for me,' he answered seriously. 'I was married, with a family to support. Young children always cramp one's style. Helen and I used to talk about what we'd be able to do once they were grown up, but of course it was only a year after Timothy went into the Navy that she died. . . Anyway,' he went on briskly, clearly not wanting to give Rosalie any chance to express her sympathy, 'my housekeeper will leave us a picnic. . .she doesn't come in on Sundays, of course. . .and I think we'll manage very well for ourselves.'

'I'm looking forward to it.'

She wasn,'t of course, but she dressed dutifully in pretty floral trousers and a cream blouse, brought her straw hat and sunglasses, and followed the directions he had given her. The house was as lovely as she had hoped, a mellow red-brick construction that seemed more civilised than her own cottage of uncompromising stone. Ivy softened the contours of the Victorian exterior and, inside, modern comforts teamed unobtrusively with tastefully chosen antiques. Collecting these pieces had been Helen Trevalley's hobby, Rosalie knew.

'Come in!' Howard said, drawing her into the large sitting-room with both hands clasping hers warmly. 'Sit down and I'll make you a cool drink. Lime cordial with soda water?'

'That sounds lovely.'

She sat down on a Nile-green *chaise-longue* and waited, studying the room. Yes, Helen's presence was still very strong here, in everything from the photos on the piano to the positioning of summery flowers in carefully chosen vases. Rosalie guessed that Howard's housekeeper, who had been with the Trevalleys part-time for years before taking on full-time duties once

Helen became ill, had simply continued to arrange everything as Helen had once ordered.

It's not like this at my place, Rosalie realised. It's so long since Mike lived there that there's almost nothing left of his touch at all. Even her photos of him were all safely arranged in albums now.

Listening to Howard clinking glasses in the kitchen, she wished he had not shown her into this room. The day was to be very casual, he had said. Wasn't there a sun-room or a shaded patio outside where they could sit? This room was too formal, and too full of Helen.

It was a relief moments later when Cathy bounced down the stairs, her blonde hair curling damply around her freckle-dappled face after a shower, and said at once, 'Oh, not in here! Where's Dad? Getting you a drink? I'll tell him we've gone out to the back terrace.'

But as they passed through the front hall there was the sound of a car, and the young doctor changed her tack, going at once to open the large wooden door. Rosalie hesitated.

'Come on,' Cathy said. 'You and Daniel go round the side of the house, and I'll help Dad with the drinks and meet you out the back. Will Daniel be happy with lime and soda, do you know?'

'I — I should think so,' Rosalie said uncertainly.

'Well, he can make do with it for now, anyway. Perhaps something stronger later on.'

And so Rosalie found herself alone with Daniel once Cathy had greeted him, pointed the way to the terrace and ducked back inside the house. It wasn't such an ordeal. He smiled and said a casual hello and they both stayed silent as they followed a brick path around the house and found the terrace. Howard and Cathy had beaten them to it, and the latter was just laying the drinks tray down on a white-painted wrought-iron table that matched a shaded circle of chairs.

As was, perhaps, natural, talk turned at once to

medical matters. 'I haven't really had a chance to talk to you about your impressions of our set-up,' Howard asked his daughter with rather endearing eagerness.

'Your set-up is very impressive, Dad,' Cathy assured him, then added with a smile that was both apologetic and mischievous, 'But from a general practitioner's point of view I think there could be more access and more communication. The telephone is right there, and a lot can be achieved by simply exchanging information between specialists and the practitioner who has often known a patient over a period of years. Actually, Daniel, I'm probably addressing this to you even more than to Dad.'

'I'll think about it,' the cardiologist promised with a lazy grin.

Meanwhile, Howard was clearly torn between disappointment and pride. Cathy never lost an opportunity to point out firmly—and usually with a hint of bold amusement—that she stood firmly in the general practitioners' camp. . .but she did it with such intelligence and style. It was easy to see why Howard was proud of her.

After a lazy half-hour, Cathy suggested that they bring the picnic things out. 'No, *not* the dining-room, Dad!' she exclaimed, forestalling his protest.

'King Lear was right,' he sighed elaborately. 'It *is* more bitter than a serpent's tooth to have a thankless child!'

'But you're not out on a blasted heath—or is that Macbeth?—you're just in too much sun. Put your chair back two feet and you'll be in the shade and Mrs Fowey's cold pork pies, with those rolls and salads, will taste heavenly out here in the fresh air, instead of the stuffy dining-room.'

I'll never be able to manage him as well as she does! Rosalie found herself thinking.

And then she was horrified. Was this the way she

should be thinking? Repentantly, she turned to
Howard.

'It *is* lovely out here, don't you think?' she smiled.

'Oh, of course,' he answered. 'I'm not really suggesting we should go in. The dining-room is a beautiful
room. Mrs Fowey set the table in there in case we
wanted to use it, but no, I agree — much nicer out
here!'

And Rosalie felt a little better after this. The meal
was delicious, too, and since their chairs were arranged
so that she didn't have to look at Daniel she was
almost able to pretend at times that he wasn't there.

'Now, there's tea and cake,' Howard said when pork
pies and salads had been consumed. 'Do you want it
now, or would you two like to go for a ride? I thought
Rosalie and I would take a ramble around the
garden. . .'

'A ride would be lovely, Dad, and I know there are
two horses waiting for us at the stables in the village,
but I don't like the look of the sky over to the west,'
Cathy replied, and her father looked in that direction.

'Oh, my goodness, yes! That's building to a thunderstorm, and they come quickly around here,' he said.
'That *is* disappointing!'

'I should be getting back fairly soon in any case,'
Daniel put in, surprising everyone, though all three
were too polite to show it.

'Tea and cake now, then?' Howard suggested.

'Well. . .time for a quick look at the garden first,'
the cardiologist conceded.

'I didn't know you were interested in gardening!'
exclaimed the surgeon, as they began to walk towards
a prettily wild south-facing slope on which grew a riot
of shrubs and flowers framed by gracious old trees.

'I'm not,' Daniel answered cheerfully. 'At least, I'm
not interested in knowing the botanical names of
hundreds of.plants. But I love the beauty of a good
garden, and I enjoy tackling a project like building a

stone wall or putting in a pond. And I like to see someone working in a garden with love. If a particular garden was blessed with such a presence, then I'd gladly help her pull out the weeds. . .'

Rosalie flushed. He might have been talking about her, and if he had been it would have been so nice, but she didn't think he was.

Howard didn't think so either. 'Yes,' he said. 'Helen did all this and I helped her in exactly that way. We used to have a gardener once a week, but that was all. Now he comes three times a week and it's not the same as having Helen's touch.'

Ashamed of herself, Rosalie took Howard's arm and squeezed it as they walked along. Daniel, sensitive and perceptive, as usual, beneath that energetic demeanour, had seen what this garden meant to Howard, and all she had been able to think of was a foolish fantasy of what might have been.

What kind of a mess am I making of my relationships with these men?' she wondered helplessly, and she focused her attention on Howard unwaveringly for the next half-hour.

But that turned out to be the wrong thing, too. Back at the house, as the growl of thunder grew louder and closer outside, Daniel and Rosalie were left alone for several minutes while Howard and Cathy went to prepare tea and cake. Rosalie was aware of the silence . . .aware, too, of tension in the air—but there was always tension before a thunderstorm.

And just then, as if to prove this, the rain came clattering on to the roof like a shower of tin cans, isolating the two of them in this still, formal room in a cocoon of violent sound.

It was then that Daniel spoke, his eyes glinting cynically as he studied her. 'So. . .seen enough to make up your mind?' There was no gentleness in him now.

'W-what do you mean?'

'Haven't you been doing a little inventory this afternoon? The house, the pool, the two acres of garden, the beautifully maintained antiques. . .'

'Are you suggesting that——?'

She broke off sharply as Howard and his daughter entered the room, each with a silver tray in hand. Anger and shocked hurt had tightened her throat unbearably and she could hardly manage to thank Cathy for the steaming Darjeeling tea in its delicate bone-china cup.

'That's a deluge out there,' Howard said.

Daniel left twenty minutes later.

CHAPTER EIGHT

'DON'T go yet,' Howard said.

Cathy had gone upstairs to pack—she was leaving first thing in the morning—and the rain had eased now. Rosalie desperately wanted to leave. She could still taste her pained response to Daniel's accusation like a bitterness in her mouth and it was terrible that the thing had been left hanging in the air. That there could be some truth to what he had said was the worst thing of all. And now Howard wanted her to prolong this awful afternoon.

'I have something to say to you.' The surgeon had come over to where she was sitting—again on the Nile-green *chaise-longue*—and had dropped to a position beside her, chafing his grey trousered knees nervously.

'Yes, Howard?' She forced herself to look up at him and found that his eyes were searching her face with troubled intensity. Her first thought—that he had chosen today to ask her to marry him—was extinguished. It couldn't be that, not with that perturbed expression on his face! And she was so confused and churned up at the moment that she didn't know whether to be glad or sorry.

'This is very hard. . .' the surgeon was saying.

'It's all right,' she assured him, still having no inkling of what this could be.

'I've realised today——' He broke off and started again. 'I've very much enjoyed our friendship, Rosalie, and I'd been hoping that perhaps it would lead to something deeper. I had thought that I would like to marry again, and that you were the kind of woman I would choose. But having you here today has made me see that it's impossible. I don't know how you feel.

148

I hope your deeper feelings haven't become involved. The thing is, I realised today that I'm still in love with Helen. I'm not ready to replace her yet, and perhaps I never will be. It's lonely here, with Timothy at sea and Cathy so busy in medicine. In many ways it would be nice to have a woman under my roof just for that reason. I always knew that I wouldn't be able to offer a new wife the love that I gave to Helen, but I had thought that companionship and respect would be enough. I see now that it wouldn't be. It would be too unfair. . .to both of us. I do hope. . .you can forgive me.'

'There's nothing to forgive,' Rosalie answered steadily and sincerely.

She knew already that she was relieved at his words, and it made sense of so much that had taken place in their awkward relationship. Unknowingly, he must always have felt the impossibility of his plan. . .

Just as I have! she realised in a blinding flash of insight. I *never* could have married Howard, even if he had felt able to replace Helen. Why have I been bashing my head against a brick wall for so long?

She saw now, very clearly — probably more clearly than he did — how both of them had been blinded and made clumsy by what they felt they *ought* to do — the way he had suggested the weekend away together, then had shrunk away from the idea, the way she had continued to accept his invitations while allowing herself to love Daniel Canaday.

To *love* him! Another blindingly clear realisation that she had no time to explore now. Her face must have registered the shock she felt at this new revelation.

'Are you sure this is all right?' Howard asked, leaning anxiously towards her.

'Very sure.' She managed a smile. 'I've enjoyed our friendship, but I didn't count on it going any further.

I'll miss our evenings together. . .at Baldwin's. . .but you haven't broken my heart, Howard.'

'Thank goodness for that!' he exclaimed, his brow clearing. 'Not that I flattered myself that. . . And you will make someone else a wonderful wife some day. I dare to hope that I might be asked to the wedding!'

'Oh, I don't think there's going to be a wedding,' Rosalie smiled thinly.

'I don't know what all those young doctors are thinking of, then,' he said with energetic gallantry.

'The young ones? They're all chasing the nursing students,' Rosalie answered, with a hollow chuckle.

'Well, I didn't mean *that* young, my dear,' he explained, surprised. 'Fellows in their forties. Mr Forster, for example.'

He had named a fellow heart surgeon who was recently divorced, and Rosalie's smile became rather fixed and forced. She considered Grant Forster, aged forty-four, to be a pompous, egotistical egghead, but he probably didn't come across that way to another surgeon. It was a cold reminder, though, that what she felt for Daniel Canaday was ludicrous. To Howard Trevalley, a man of forty-four, not thirty-two, was suitable for Rosalie. Dr Canaday, after all, was the man he had earmarked for his daughter.

'I really should go,' she said distractedly.

'Yes, of course. Cathy will be down again soon and she'll wonder what's going on if we've still got our heads together like this. I'm. . .very glad you understand, my dear. I only hope. . . Well, we've kept the thing pretty much a secret, but I hope our friendship hasn't—er—kept you out of circulation.'

'No, it hasn't,' she answered thoughtlessly, her mind on Daniel. Then, realising how this sounded, she added hastily, 'I mean, it hasn't been a problem. I haven't felt——'

'Good, good, that's understood, then.' He was becoming flustered now too, and both of them were eager for the afternoon to be over. They had risen and were edging out of the room. 'Shall I call Cathy down to say goodbye?'

'No, don't interrupt her. I expect she has a lot to do. Just wish her the best of luck on my behalf in her new job, will you?'

'Of course.'

'And thank you for a lovely day. The garden is beautiful. What a pity our exploration was interrupted by the storm!'

And this brought them both to the door. Minutes later, Rosalie was steering her small car down the curved gravel driveway. She turned out of it and into the quiet road that led to the small nearby village of Dulverham, but before she had gone more than a few hundred yards she was overcome by a trembling in her hands that forced her to pull over to the side of the road, switch off the engine and wait for the weakness to subside.

Daniel. . . That was what this was about. The knowledge that she could not marry Howard was nothing compared to the full knowledge of her feelings for the cardiologist, although the two realisations were inextricably linked.

'I knew I was emotionally involved,' she whispered into the hot hands that were pressed against her mouth. Her brown eyes, dry and burning, stared unseeingly ahead to where the stone wall that bordered the road curved away to the right. 'But I kept thinking that it was a trick my body was playing. It's not a trick! It's real, and it's hopeless! I should have risked everything. . .slept with him. . .taken every moment I could get even if it didn't last. I don't love him because he's offering safety and convention. If I'd wanted that, then I would have loved Howard and I'd have been hurt today at what he said. I love Daniel because he *doesn't* offer convention and safety. He dares me to. . . He *dared* me,' she corrected firmly, 'to open up my life to

new things, to act impulsively and to think and feel
more fully. Why couldn't I have let that be enough?'

For a moment she considered going to him to offer
. . .whatever he wanted—a crazy, sensual affair, some
wild heedless weekend together before one or both of
them moved on to new pastures. But it was too late to
offer that now. Very possibly he was involved with
Cathy Trevalley—a woman to whom such lack of
convention would probably come more naturally, and
a woman, too, who would make a better candidate for
marriage if, in the end, he did want to settle down,
because she would be able to give him children. . .

Perhaps this way I'm saving myself from pain later
on. That's the best way to think of it. The *only* way,
Rosalie decided wearily after a long time.

The rain had completely stopped now and the sun
had come out again, with none of this morning's
oppressive quality to its warmth. Droplets of water
still sparkled on the frenzied foliage that grew over the
ancient Cornish stone walls that bordered the road-
side, and there was a delicious freshness in the air.

At home her roses would be starting to lift their
heavy, sodden petals to the light once more. It was
time to go.

'My stint on this ward is coming to an end,' Elise Jones
said, apparently to no one in particular, and apropos
of nothing special.

'Yes, I suppose it is,' Rosalie answered vaguely. The
summer had passed quickly, it seemed. Jackie Billings
was back down here under her care, and would soon
be ready to go home, and many other patients had
come and gone. . . But then when she thought back to
the beginning of the summer and realised that it was
then that her involvement with Daniel Canaday had
started she decided that it hadn't passed quickly at all.

But it seemed that it was the cardiologist who lay
behind Elise's words as well. She added on a flamboy-

ant sigh, 'Which means I'll never see that gorgeous
man again.'

The man in question had just come into the ward
briefly to look at a new patient and was now on his
way out again. He had tossed a brief greeting to
Rosalie when he passed the nurses' station on his way
in, and now he tossed her a brief goodbye as he left. It
was typical of the exchanges she and Daniel had had
over the five weeks since that emotional day at
Howard's.

His gaze seemed to skate away from her whenever
possible. He would look down at his hands or at a
patient, over at a clock or an open doorway — anywhere but at her. Rosalie felt that everyone must
notice their awkwardness, but no one did, just as no
one had noticed during those heady weeks when black
eyes had met brown ones and held constantly, creating
threads of fiery awareness.

'Bye, Dr Canaday,' Elise called after the departing
cardiologist, and he turned briefly to smile back at her.
Rosalie quickly bent her head to a patient's file in front
of her, thankful that she was on the phone. She had
been put on hold several minutes ago by Admissions,
of course, and was still waiting, but Daniel wasn't to
know that, as she gave every appearance of nodding
and listening intently down the line. Seconds later he
was safely out of sight.

'You and your silly crushes, Elise!' exclaimed
Beverly Moore, passing by on her way to a filing
drawer.

'It's not silly,' Elise answered seriously. 'I know I
could never get a man like him really interested.
Instead, I simply lust after him openly and that takes
the pressure off. Much better than crying into my
pillow and dreaming rosy fantasies every night.'

'Hmm,' Beverly said, but Rosalie thought that
she detected a faint pinkening of the other
woman's cheeks.

Don't tell me Beverly has a crush on him as well! she thought. She sees him at meetings for the heart care project. Perhaps she's hoping. . .

It made her own feelings seem more tarnished and vulnerable, but she supposed they would fade in time. That seemed the only possible way out. Meanwhile, there was work to do. It was eight o'clock on Friday evening, and time to check on her patients now that visiting hour — a quiet one tonight — had finished. Daniel must be on call, she realised. He didn't usually come in this late otherwise. . .

The shift continued uneventfully. Outside, it was raining and had been all day. Rosalie could hear the gutters running outside the windows and when she glanced out into the gathering night she saw that the bitumen expanse of the car park was glistening and black, broken in parts by long reflections of light from nearby buildings.

At about ten o'clock, she made one of her frequent and regular visits to Mr Slade's bedside. He had been with them for a long time now, after the surgery that had successfully drained his pericardium. For a while he had seemed to be recovering well, and there was talk of sending him home, but then his condition had begun to deteriorate again. His heart-rate was slowing gradually, and occasionally there were missed or abnormal beats. Ventrical tachycardia, it was called.

Mr Slade had become depressed after such a long hospital stay. He was a widower, and his children lived a distance away and had only managed one visit each over the summer. Now, Rosalie had been told during the ward conference earlier this afternoon at the change of shift, he had a low-grade fever. He was hooked up to permanent monitoring, and his heart rhythm could be seen at a glance while at the nurses' station, but Rosalie always preferred to look at the real patient, not just his condition as symbolised by lines of light on a screen.

He seemed to be sleeping, she found, as she stood at his bedside, so she did not disturb him, just looked for a few minutes — that look she had recognised on Daniel's face more than once, *willing* a patient to get well — then tiptoed away again. Behind her as she left his private room, she heard him move weakly and restlessly, and felt a sense of foreboding that was not long in bearing its sad fruit.

Before she even arrived back at the nurses' station, she heard the warning pip of the monitor. There were four patients connected to EKGs at the moment, but Mr Slade's was the first she looked at, and this time she knew that it was more than just a short episode of ventrical tachycardia. In other words, his heart rhythm was completely wrong. She paged the emergency team immediately, knowing as she did so that Daniel Canaday would probably be among them.

He was. As usual, the team erupted on to the ward impossibly quickly, and the next period of time was disjointed, urgent and confusing. Mr Slade's heart was showing sustained ventrical tachycardia now, and fibrillation as well. Daniel Canaday acted and gave orders with commanding efficiency. The patient was intubated and given oxygen, an IV line was inserted and medication bombarded his system — ligocaine, ephinephrine, sodium bicarbonate.

'Still no pulse,' Daniel said. 'Let's try this again.' And again the paddles of the defibrillator were pressed to Mr Slade's inert chest.

It was a long time before they finally gave up. Then a different team of staff took over, and Mr Slade was taken away. Daniel had remained after the emergency team left, as it was his responsibility to pronounce formally that life was extinguished.

'Well, I think we all knew it was on the cards,' he said quietly and sadly to Rosalie after it was all over. 'It happens. And I tell myself that I've chosen a speciality where it is going to keep on happening so I'd better get used to it. . . But it's never easy.'

'I know.'

'He was a high-risk patient from the beginning, and he made a good fight. Perhaps we never should have attempted surgery in the first place.'

'In that case. . .well, the end result would have been the same,' Rosalie reminded him. 'Without surgery he certainly didn't have long to live.'

'I'll call his family. From my office, I think. Then I'll be off home. It's just chance that I was in here tonight. I'm only second on call, and that ends at midnight. But things have been busy. Somehow it already seems like a very long night.' He began to walk away.

'You did everything you could, Daniel,' she reassured him once again, and he turned to her.

'So did you.' Then he was gone.

Rosalie shrugged arms and shoulders into her raincoat and wrestled with a recalcitrant umbrella. Her car sat rather forlornly by itself on the far side of the car park. That was the worst of an evening shift. When she arrived at three, the place was always nearly full, and she could never get a decent space.

She stepped out from the shelter of the hospital's entranceway and began the hurried journey across the bitumen. Her stockings were soon splashed with water and the damp air chilled her face and hands. Three hours ago, watching the rain from the ward, it had seemed benign enough, but now, after what had just happened, it had taken on a quality of mournfulness.

Reaching her car, Rosalie fumbled for the keys in her bag, cursing herself for not getting them out while she was still under shelter. At last she found them and slipped behind the wheel. It would be good to be home! She put the key in the ignition, turned it. . .and nothing happened. She tried again. Still nothing. Knowing enough about cars to realise that it was

probably a problem with the battery and that therefore
it was useless to keep trying, Rosalie slumped in her
seat for a moment. *Not* what she needed tonight, of all
nights!

I'll have to go back inside and call a garage. . .
although who will be open at this time of night. . .
Perhaps I'd better just get a taxi and deal with it
tomorrow.

Wearily, she climbed from the vehicle again and felt
a hiss of droplets against her legs as another car passed.
Turning angrily, she found that the vehicle, which she
recognised, had stopped. It was Daniel.

'What's the matter?'

'Flat battery, I think. Or a short circuit in it. Who
knows?'

'Get in, then.' He leaned across to open his passen-
ger door for her and she climbed in without another
word. On a night like tonight there was no sense in
being difficult. And anyway, she felt closer to him
after tonight's quiet tragedy than she had for weeks. It
was a relief to be with someone who would feel as
little in the mood for light conversation as she did.

'What time are you due in tomorrow?' he asked
after their blessed, peaceful silence had lasted for
several minutes.

'Three. Which is good,' she said. 'I'll be able to
organise a mechanic to come and look at it.'

'Not a fun way to spend your morning.'

'I know. But these things happen.'

'They do.'

Silence fell again, and it remained unbroken until
they had almost reached her house. Then, as if seizing
a chance that might not come again, Daniel said,
'Rosalie, while we're together like this I want to
apologise for what I said to you at Howard Trevalley's
that day.'

'Oh. . .'

'You know what I mean?'

'Yes.'

'It's not true. I knew it wasn't true even when I said it.'

'Then why did you?'

'Because I was angry with you.'

There was a pause, then Rosalie said quietly, 'But what you said *was* true, partly, Daniel. At least, I *wanted* Howard's house and his beautiful antiques to make a difference. I wanted them to help me decide to marry him.'

'And have you decided that?' he asked neutrally. 'Are you going to marry him?'

'No, I'm not.' At that moment they pulled up outside her gate, and before she could question the idea Rosalie found herself suggesting, 'Why don't you come in and have some hot chocolate? I'm sure you need it. We both do.'

'All right. I'd like that.'

They were silent once again as they entered the house. She turned on the lights and went to the kitchen while he switched on an electric heater as the damp day had brought a chill to the cottage now that it was so late at night.

Whether it was that she was emotionally drained after tonight's sad drama, or whether it was the quietly honest conversation in the car, Rosalie didn't know, but she did know that something was making her feel more at ease with Daniel tonight. When she had made the hot chocolate and brought it in to him, they sat together on the couch, holding the thick mugs in their hands to warm chilly fingers and sipping appreciatively, still in a silence that felt. . .nice.

It was only as he put down his empty mug with an expressive sigh that Daniel leaned back on the comfortable couch and said, 'So you're not going to marry Howard.'

'No.'

'Was it a mutual decision?'

'Yes, I think it was,' she answered cautiously, and then something impelled her to be completely honest. 'I'd made up my mind that I *would* marry him, then he found that he was still in love with Helen and couldn't ask me, and I discovered I was very relieved.'

'Why?'

But this she could not answer honestly. It would betray her too nakedly. Instead, she said, 'I thought I wanted security and safety — a relationship that everyone would think suitable, no one would be too surprised or shocked at. But I found out that I was wrong.'

'Did you find out what you wanted instead?'

She laughed softly and a little wearily. 'You're not afraid of asking the hard questions, are you?'

'No, but you needn't feel obliged to answer them,' he smiled back.

And then, without her quite knowing how it had happened, his arm came around her and he coaxed her glossy head to lie against the firm, cradling shape of his shoulder and they sat there without moving or speaking for quite some time. It reminded her of that night at the ballet after Jackie Billings's transplant — tranquil, reassuring, warm. . .

But even as she thought this something in the quality of their contact began to change. He shifted a little on the couch so that they were facing each other now, and his hands began to caress her gently.

He had not yet touched her lips, but now he reached behind him and switched off the table lamp that had brightened the room, so that only the orange glow of the electric fire fell on them. Next he slipped his fingers into her hair and shook out the combs and clips that had confined it during the day so that it all fell around her shoulders in a rich red halo. Rosalie protested against none of this. She knew that she was going to give herself to him tonight, emotionally as well as physically, and she wanted it more than she had ever wanted anything.

'Is this all right?' he murmured with a soft sighing hiss in her ear.

'Yes,' came her unhesitating answer.

It was ironic that it was Howard who had led her to this point, at least in part. He had shown her the futility of trying to engineer one's destiny with one's brain when the heart knew so much better. The clamouring voice of the surgeon's heart had finally told his slower, stubborner mind that Helen was still too important to him, and now it was time for Rosalie to listen to the voice of her own much misunderstood emotional organ.

It's silly, she thought hazily. I work with heart patients all day. I shouldn't have been this slow to know. . .

But of course it wasn't the same thing at all. Calling it her 'heart' was just a convenience. It was *all* of her that knew now how much she loved Daniel and how freely she had to give herself to this night no matter what it might cost, instead of protecting herself, as she had been doing, with the staid familiarity of the life she had known before Daniel had come into her world and set it on fire.

These thoughts came to her almost without inner words, and soon she was not thinking at all, only feeling and experiencing. Daniel spent timeless minutes coaxing uniform and pale silky undergarments from her body, while her own fingers rediscovered the lost knowledge of how it felt to undress a man. Eventually they lay naked together, resting temporarily from a sensuousness that was already dangerous in its intensity of passion.

As she lay entwined with him, Rosalie could feel how right it was, how perfectly her soft curves shaped themselves into the harder, less tender planes of his figure. She felt the pulsing weight of her full breasts brushing against the light, slightly scratchy hair of his chest, and the capable length of his thighs tightened against her own, and knew that there was an even more intimate fit of maleness to femaleness that she would soon discover.

It was a *rediscovery*, of course, but somehow it didn't feel that way. Mike was so long ago, she had changed so much since then. . .and Daniel was such a very different kind of man. Without any disloyalty to Mike, she knew that Daniel had far more to offer the woman she was now. She had been scarcely more than a child nineteen years ago on that nervous bridal night, and now she was a seasoned woman knowing a little tenativeness about what was to come, but no real fear.

The moments of quiescence were over now. Both felt their urgency rise to the surface once more, and soon he was bathing her shoulders, neck, breasts with hot kisses that made her own mouth hunger for him desperately. The landscape of their interlocked bodies was blurred and softened by the diffuse orange glow of the electric fire, and now the timescape of the night blurred and softened as well. She could not have described, even to herself, the steps that led to their climactic mutual fulfilment, only knowing — as it happened and afterwards — that each moment was right in every way.

His groans of ecstasy were wrenched from deep within him, matching her own cries, and neither of them held back from the animal expression of all that they felt. Afterwards came a time that was as wonderful in its way as what had just happened. They lay together again, neither making any attempt to move or speak as their pulses slowed and their limbs relaxed in perfect comfort and warmth.

At last he sighed and stirred. 'Can we go to bed?' he whispered.

'Bed?'

'Yes. Not a coy way of saying. . .what we just did. I

mean literally. I want to hold you, and to fall asleep in your arms. . .for the rest of the night.'

'Yes. . .'

He helped her up and pushed her ahead of him with light fingertips on her back. In the darkness, neither of them made any attempt to gather their clothes. On the stairs, away from the heat of the electric fire, whose 'off' switch he had flicked briefly on his way past, the chill struck on her skin. She felt it tightening her back and her still achingly sensitive breasts, and was glad that there was a summer-weight padded quilt on the bed. To hold Daniel, or to be held by him all night as they slept. . .!

When they reached her room she was still walking ahead of him, and felt his warm hands soothing the chilly air from her back and then slip around to explore the soft curves of her hips before climbing upwards to find and cup the taut globes of her breasts. They each gave a shuddering sigh and sank on to the bed, peeling back the covers then pulling them up again so that they were cocooned in warmth as well as darkness now.

It seemed like no more than a minute before she had drifted into a dreamily smiling sleep. . .and no more than five minutes before she awakened again, knowing instinctively from the feel of her own body and of his that they were ready to discover each other's most passionate responses once again.

This time it was even more relaxed and gentle, and even more right — if that could be. They talked and teased a little, too — silly, ephemeral things, mostly, that could never be enshrined even in memory. And when, once again, the wave of their desire had crashed and broken on the shore of release, the sleep they fell into was even deeper and more complete.

CHAPTER NINE

ROSALIE stirred, sighed, smiled and slipped back into a half-sleep, hugging the pretty, cream-patterned sheets around bare skin that felt deliciously alive and at the same time utterly relaxed. She had some reason for being incredibly happy, she realised drowsily. For the moment, she couldn't remember what it was, but that didn't matter. She would just enjoy it. And then she did remember, which felt even better. Last night . . .and Daniel.

With eyes still buttoned shut by sleep, she rolled over and reached out for the warmth of his back, already so familiar and right in this bed, it seemed.

He wasn't there. Her eyes flew open. No, her eager hands had not deceived her. The bed beside her was empty, only the imprint of his head on the pillow and the rumpled sheets telling her that he had ever been there at all. She pulled the top sheet back a little and pressed her palm to the bed. Still faintly warm. He had not been gone for very long.

He must be downstairs, she decided, and, already eager to see him again, she jumped out of bed and slid into a summery kimono of Chinese flowered silk. Its bright peacock-blue background clashed ridiculously with her hair and always had, but she didn't care. Forgetting vanity, she didn't even brush the passion-tangled locks, but hurried downstairs in search of him, pausing only at the bottom when she realised that the place was silent.

Daniel was not in the house. She knew that now and a glance out of the window confirmed it. His car had gone. Had he been called out? No, she remembered. His on-call period had ended at midnight. Perhaps

there was an emergency. Had he left a note? Madly,
she searched the house, then had to laugh bitterly — at
herself. After exhausting the two or three obvious
places, she had started a search as thorough as if she
had been a child playing hunt the thimble.

She thought of another possibility — a little French
delicatessen had opened up in the next village. Something of a tourist trap, it none the less sold delicious
croissants. Perhaps he had noticed it and had gone to
buy some for breakfast. It was the kind of thing he
might do, she decided, allowing a warm smile and a
warm feeling to envelop her at last.

In which case, he should be back at any minute.
Quickly, she put coffee on the stove to brew and got
out a bright Italian coffee set that had large round cups
and generous-sized plates. She laid table mats and
cutlery on the small table in the breakfast-room, which
caught the morning sun beautifully on a day like today,
and squeezed some fresh orange juice as well. Butter
and jam, milk and sugar. It was all ready.

And Daniel should have been back by now. Looking
at the clock she saw that it was a quarter to ten, and
she had first awoken at nine. Even if he had only just
left the house, and even if he had struck a crowd in
the French delicatessen, the errand should not have
taken more than half an hour.

I'm a fool, she realised, her spirits deflating like a
balloon. He's not buying croissants, or flowers, or the
newspaper, or anything else. He's just *gone* that's all,
and I've read enough problem columns in women's
magazines to know what *that* means!

A one-night stand. It was what she had been afraid
of all along. Last night, she would have sworn that it
was not like this for him. For both of them it had
seemed so right, and the way he had held her as they
slept after their passion was spent had made her
believe that he felt more for her than mere physical

need. But this morning's vanishing act was pretty cold, hard evidence that she had been wrong.

After waiting another vain half-hour, Rosalie cleared the pretty breakfast setting away. She had no appetite now. By one o'clock, after only some summer fruit to eat, she was in quite a state, and it was only then that she remembered her car, parked forlorn and unfunctioning at the hospital. No time left to organise a garage mechanic to come and look at it — barely time to pull on her uniform and hurry for the slow bus that came winding through the village every two hours. Oh, if this was the aftermath of a casual affair, she never wanted to experience it again, and wished very badly that she was not experiencing it now.

She found work tiring and stressful. Snatching a spare moment shortly after she arrived, she rang a garage and they promised to send someone out. This, at least, was done promptly and she handed over her car keys absently. They were returned to her by the gruff young mechanic only a few minutes later.

'Your battery was out of water,' he reported. 'No trouble to fix. But I'll have to charge you for my time, since I had to come up from the garage like this.'

'You mean it's fixed?' queried Rosalie blankly.

'It's fixed all right.'

Automatically, she wrote out the modest cheque and the man went on his way. Ironic to think that it had been such a small thing, and if it hadn't happened, then neither might last night. . .with Daniel. . .have taken place.

The cardiologist had not been in this afternoon, and she supposed she was grateful for that. . .although the red-headed streak in her personality would have liked to confront him, to see his face and force him to meet her eye. . .if he could.

It wasn't until just before her evening meal break that she heard Elise say casually to Beverly Moore, 'Oh, Dr Canaday's not going to be in again till

Monday, apparently. He's sick, or something. There's a message on the pad about it. It's in Sister Blair's writing, so of course I could barely read it. He phoned at about half-past one, it says. Or no, *he* didn't phone, someone else phoned for him. I don't know. . .'

'Well, it doesn't matter,' Beverly answered. .

'Did you have a problem with one of Dr Canaday's patients, Beverly?' Rosalie put in reluctantly.

'No, just a question about the next heart care project meeting,' the other nurse answered, saying the last words a little possessively. 'It's really not important.'

'Elise, do you know who *is* handling his patients if there's a problem? Does the message say?' Rosalie asked now. She felt as if she should be the one to know the answer to this question, but she had been struggling to get on top of things this afternoon, and low-priority tasks like flipping through the message pad hadn't yet got to the top of her list.

'Um—no, I don't think so,' the girl answered. 'I was just—er—looking for a personal message from a friend. I gave him this number and he said he might ring. I wasn't really——'

'May I look at the pad, please?' Rosalie said wearily, holding out her hand for it. The junior nurse passed it quickly across the desk, and Rosalie flipped the pages till she came to Megan Blair's untidy scrawl.

'Sat. 1.30 p.m. Dr Canaday ill. In Monday. Meanwhile, Dr Parkinson. Contact: Sr Harriet Croft,' was all it said, and all was quite clear to Rosalie—although she didn't really believe that he was ill—except the last part. Who was Sister Harriet Croft? Not a familiar name at this hospital, certainly, unless she was new. Or perhaps it didn't say 'Sr', perhaps it said 'Ms', or even 'Dr'. Megan's writing really was impossible.

'We page Dr Parkinson if any of Dr Canaday's patients have a problem,' she reported to Beverly. 'Can you write that down *clearly* on the white-board for the other shifts? Not that I think there will be any problems that the on-call doctors can't cover, but still. . .'

'Dr Parkinson will probably make a round tomorrow morning, won't he?' Beverly queried.

'I should think so.'

And that was the end of the subject as far as everyone else was concerned. Rosalie could not stop thinking about it, of course, and she had to conclude that he wasn't really ill at all, that he was simply staying away—even at the price of neglecting his patients over the weekend—so that they didn't have to face each other again too soon. She couldn't decide if that was faintly considerate of him, or if it was the cruellest cut of all.

The knocking at the front door prodded Rosalie from a late Sunday morning sleep in which frankly she had been hiding to postpone the thoughts of Daniel that just would not go away. Stumbling around the bedroom, she found yesterday's peacock-blue kimono and put it on—only today there was a white cotton nightdress beneath it, instead of yesterday's bare, sensuously fulfilled curves of flesh. She had slept badly, only dropping into deeper slumber at dawn, and she already felt irritated at the prospect of boys selling raffle tickets for their cricket club, or whatever this knocking might mean.

It was Daniel. He almost fell through the door into her arms straight away, squashing a bag of what felt like. . .*croissants* between them. It was as if the whole of yesterday had been a dream—or a nightmare—and he had, after all, simply gone to the French delicatessen to bring home breakfast.

For one bewildered moment, Rosalie decided that it *had* been a dream, that he had got beneath her skin so thoroughly that she didn't even know what reality was any more, but then reason reasserted itself.

And then he spoke, his arms around her although

she was struggling to free herself from his embrace. 'God, Rosalie! This has been a nightmare!'

She felt hysterical laughter rising in her throat as she finally succeeded in pushing him away. 'It certainly has!' Her voice was cold, and it was trembling. Then her hysteria broke the surface. 'And now you're going to try to explain it, I presume? Well, you've had twenty-four hours to think up something so I dare say it will be quite convincing. What really happened? Things didn't look so rosy and simple in broad daylight, I suppose, and you couldn't face breakfast. There wasn't much point in bothering with, "Goodbye," I dare say. After all, you'd already got what you wanted, hadn't you? I'm not sure why you're here now, but I expect you'll tell me. I might even be fool enough to believe it, too!'

It was a wild outburst, more full of naked emotion and hurt than anything she had ever said before. In the back of her mind, she had just enough control left to think, so this is what love does when it comes in tandem with such passion! I was crazy to think I could handle life at this speed!

Daniel was standing rigidly, his eyes narrowed as he listened to her. She could scarcely bear to look at him, but was dimly aware that there was something different about his appearance this morning. He had drawn a hissing breath at the close of her tumbling speech, but for a long moment he didn't attempt to reply, and the silence was thick and hard between them. When he finally did speak, it was heavy and regretful.

'I can't stand this, Rosalie.'

'You can't stand what?' she retorted, crisply and impatiently.

'For a start, must we have this conversation on your front porch?'

'What? Oh. . .' She had forgotten that they were still standing at the door.

Daniel had brushed past her now. She saw that he

was heading for the kitchen, and followed him. He dumped the bag of croissants on the polished counter-top then turned away from them impatiently. 'I won't stay,' he said. 'But you might as well have those. I was going to make breakfast for us, but. . . I can't now.'

'I don't understand.'

'I came to apologise. . .and explain. . .and to laugh about it with you.'

'Laugh?'

'I'd hoped so, yes. I'd also hoped for some sympathy!' He touched a hand to his temple and only now did Rosalie register the fact that a square inch or two of his black hair had been shaved away and a flesh-coloured dressing applied in its place.

'Daniel!'

'I crept out yesterday morning to buy us some croissants for breakfast. I hoped you'd stay asleep. But I never made it to the shop. Another car went through a stop sign and ploughed into me. I was unconscious for several minutes and an ambulance took me to the local cottage hospital. They stitched my head and diagnosed concussion, made me stay in hospital for twenty-four hours. I've only just discharged myself, by the way, and a little sooner than they would have liked. Yesterday, by the time I was oriented enough to ring you here, you'd left so I left a message at the hospital, then conked out again, pretty much. Slept the rest of the day and felt fairly rotten. Didn't dare to make the message too personal but I *did* think it was an acceptable explanation for my absence. Obviously you disagreed.'

'It just said. . . Megan Blair wrote it down. . .you were ill. I thought you were running away! Oh, Daniel!' She went to him and tried to hold him, wanting to kiss the bruises that spread from beneath the dressing on his face, but he held her at arm's length.

'No, Rosalie.' It was gentle but very firm.

'What's wrong?'

He turned from her, laughed ruefully, paced the room a little. 'You were pretty angry just then. On Friday night, things were different. We seemed to understand each other. . .'

Now it was her turn for laughter that contained a hint of bitter complexity. 'Oh, in that area we've never had any trouble communicating!'

'I don't just mean *bed*!' He said the word bluntly and easily. 'I mean. . . But why bother to go into it? That's the whole problem. I'd hoped Friday night was a fresh start for us, but I think I was kidding myself, because things are just the same as they've always been, aren't they? I won't say it's your fault. Perhaps it's me. Perhaps I should just bulldoze through your doubts, but I can't. I want——' But he broke off and didn't finish, turning to face her again and spreading his hands in a gesture of helplessness. 'I think I should go.'

'All right,' was all her lips could manage. Even now she yearned to respond to him in some more dramatic way, to match the painful honesty of his words, but she couldn't. He was right. She still had too many doubts. She didn't trust their relationship enough to tell him she loved him, and that was the only really honest thing she had to say.

'And Rosalie?' He was already at the kitchen door, heading to walk down the passage and out the front.

'Yes?'

'Much as I enjoyed that hot chocolate together on Friday night. . .let's not do that sort of thing again. It's too hard for both of us, in the circumstances, don't you think?'

And there she had no trouble agreeing with him.

'Well, *that's* bad news,' Beverly Moore said expressively as she put down the phone sharply on a Wednesday morning in early September.

'What is?' Rosalie asked, arriving at the nurses' station after completing the morning medication round with the help of a newer junior, Jaimie Stivell.

'We're getting Norman Goodheart back!'

'Ohh. . .!' Rosalie couldn't help the elaborate groan.

It must be months now since Mr Goodheart had been discharged. Usually, it was hard to remember a patient after so long, but no one had any trouble remembering this one. The irony of his name tended to engrave itself upon the memory, for a start. The man did *not* have a good heart, either physically or emotionally. He had had bypass surgery, as his left main artery was eighty-five per cent blocked, and both before and after the surgery he had been one of the most cantankerous patients Rosalie had ever encountered.

'What's the problem this time?' she asked Beverly.

'Oh, the same old chest pain, apparently. Just as bad as before the bypass, so he says. Casualty haven't done anything much with him. They're just passing the buck straight to us, I think. Dr Canaday is doing angioplasties this morning, but I gather he'll be up here to examine our old friend in an hour or so. He's in for a treat! Do you think we should warn him?'

'Warn him? Oh, of course, he hadn't started here in March, had he? I forgot,' Rosalie answered somewhat woodenly. It was always hard for her these days to remember that Daniel had only been at St Bede's for a comparatively short time.

'No, he started in May,' Beverly answered, a little smile on her face, and again Rosalie wondered if Staff Nurse Moore had tender feelings for the cardiologist.

It was nearly three weeks since that explosive morning at her cottage and nothing had changed. Both of them took pains to keep out of each other's way.

He could be going out with Beverly, or with Cathy Trevalley, Rosalie realised. I couldn't know. I couldn't ever guess from his face, because I try so hard not to look at him now.

Only a few minutes later, Mr Goodheart arrived on the ward, escorted in a wheelchair by an orderly as all admissions were. Rosalie was still busy frantically readjusting her bed arrangements. Mr Goodheart simply *had* to have a private room. There was no grounds for it medically, unless you counted the fact that if he was in with other patients none of them would ever get better, but it would certainly help the nursing staff by reducing the number of things he had to complain about!

'We'll have to put Mr Green in with Mr Taylor,' she told Beverly. 'Then Mr Bevan can go in the four-bed room across the corridor and we'll have Number Five for Mr Goodheart.'

'I need something for this pain at once!' were Mr Goodheart's first words as he entered the ward, and the orderly departed with evident relief, leaving the man sitting in his wheelchair.

'Didn't they give you anything in Casualty?' Rosalie wanted to know.

'No!' he snapped. 'Or I wouldn't be asking, would I? And it's like a sword being lanced through my chest.'

'What about your nitroglycerine? Have you still been taking that?'

'Totally useless!' he snapped again. 'Didn't bother to bring it with me. Why haven't I been placed in Intensive Care?'

After what seemed like an inordinate length of time, the new patient was finally ensconced in bed with as much medication as Rosalie could safely administer without a doctor's say-so. Not much, unfortunately. It would probably be another half-hour before Daniel Canaday arrived. For a moment she considered paging another doctor just for the sake of some peace, but if Mr Goodheart was to be Dr Canaday's patient. . .

Rosalie wasn't feeling terribly well today, she

realised, but it was nothing she could put a name to. A little fatigued, a little vague, a little bloated and crampy. Shrugging it off, she promised herself a quiet afternoon and evening after her working day ended at three. Just a lazy hour or two reading a book in the garden and drinking tea, a simple supper, a warm, soothing bath and early to bed. What a pity it wasn't time to hand over to the in-coming shift for several more hours!

I don't usually count the hours at work like this, she realised. I really must be unwell. A low-grade virus, or something.

Daniel Canaday arrived at last, and went to examine the new admission without delay. It seemed to take him a long time, and Rosalie wasn't surprised when he sought her out at another patient's bedside and summoned her back to the relative privacy of the nurses' station.

'I've scheduled a catheterisation for tomorrow morning,' he said, 'although I'm not convinced that any of his grafts have closed. I've also prescribed every possible medication — at his insistence. Please police him very carefully. I think he's been taking too many pain-killers at home.'

'I wouldn't be surprised,' Rosalie agreed.

'Can you give me some history on him?'

'Can we ever!' Beverly exclaimed in the background. She was hovering there, ostensibly studying some charts, but Rosalie suspected that she wanted to be included in the conversation.

As there was no reason why she should not be, Rosalie moved her chair a little so that the younger woman became part of the triangle and said, 'Beverly knows just as much about him as I do, and I don't think she'd bother to mince words either — he's a very difficult patient!'

'I gathered that. . .'

'He complains about *everything*. Noise, pain, hospital odours and other patients' habits.'

'Hmm. He's put on weight since his discharge, and he admitted that he's smoking again. I'm not sure what he wants to hear after the catheterisation tomorrow. If the grafts have closed, it'll mean angioplasty at the very least, and that's just a temporary solution if he won't make any changes at home. I hate these readmissions,' he said, quite harshly. 'We've only just discharged Mr Robinson after his bypass, and I suspect he's another patient who won't do the work at home. His GP. . .'

'Dr Eltham.'

'That's right. . . He says Robinson's work and home life are as stressful as ever, and he suspects there'll be no co-operation with diet and exercise.'

'Dr Canaday,' Beverly put in, pink-cheeked, 'I had an idea.'

'Yes?'

'It involves the heart care project. Should I. . .?'

'Yes, bring it up at the next meeting,' he said offhandedly. Rosalie could see that, having got his feelings about Mr Goodheart off his chest, he was anxious to get on with his work, but Beverly was not so perceptive.

'Oh, no, I mean it's about Mr Goodheart.'

'I thought you said——'

'No, him *and* the heart care project. I wondered if we should go somewhere private to discuss it.' She didn't look at Rosalie, but the latter felt excluded. Fortunately, she was able to take it in her stride. Beverly had been growing *quite* possessive about the heart care project lately, adding further evidence to the idea that she had rather a serious crush on its chairman.

'The heart care project isn't confidential in any way, Beverly,' Dr Canaday was saying now.

'Oh, of course not. I just. . . Never mind. You see,

I thought Mr Goodheart might make a good volunteer. At least, you know how we need volunteers now at the lower levels to get involved in giving out pamphlets and so on? I thought if he was co-opted it might help him to see how relevant it is to his own life.'

'It's an idea,' the cardiologist said tactfully. 'I'm not sure that Mr Goodheart is the sort of person who'd respond in that way, from what I've just heard.' He flicked Rosalie a quick glance and saw that she agreed with him, while she in her turn was poignantly aware that this was the closest moment of communication they had had in three weeks.

Beverly evidently *didn't* see that she was only being humoured in her proposal. 'It's worth a try, though, isn't it?' she urged enthusiastically. 'I mean, just from what you were saying at the last meeting. It made so much sense. About——'

'Thanks, yes, that's good to hear. I'll think about Mr Goodheart, and we'll see what tomorrow's procedure shows up. Bye, Rosalie.'

'Bye.' Both women echoed the word. Rosalie, studying Beverly covertly, saw that the younger woman was hiding her face over her case-notes, obviously disappointed by what had happened.

He *can't* be involved with her!

The realisation was a relief. . .until Rosalie questioned this reaction in herself. She felt a little sorry for Beverly, and in any case her problem with Daniel was not a rival, it was basic incompatability, which nothing could change. Daniel had realised this, and seemed to be taking it easily in his stride. Why can't I be realistic about it in the same way? she wondered.

By the end of the shift, all the nursing staff were feeling very *unrealistic* in their hopes about Mr Goodheart. They either wanted a miracle cure to take place *now* so that he could be discharged, or they wanted tomorrow's cardiac catheterisation to reveal a major and very, very rare problem that would necessitate sending him off to a team of experts on the other side of the Atlantic.

Unfortunately, Rosalie knew that neither of these things was likely to happen. Experience and knowledge of human nature told her that Daniel Canaday's diagnosis was all too likely to be correct — the bypass in February had been successful, and it was only the patient's refusal to make changes in his life and view the situation positively that was causing his continued pain and poor quality of life.

At home, feeling utterly weary, she didn't even attempt her plan to sit in the garden with a book, although it was a beautiful September day. Instead, she slumped into the bathroom and ran a hot bath, then hesitated over several different kinds of scented bath oils and salts. Lemon verbena was always nice. Opening the packet of salts and smelling it appreciatively, she expected to enjoy the familiar fragrance in her nostrils. Instead, however, she was assailed by a sudden, almost overwhelming nausea.

I won't have a scented bath after all, she decided quickly. The nausea soon subsided with no disastrous consequences, but, lolling in the plain hot water minutes later, she concluded that she really must have some kind of low-grade ailment. This relaxing water was almost sending her to sleep, and when the bath was finished she *did* sleep, for two hours, to awaken feeling so refreshed and well and alive that she decided she couldn't be ill after all.

Is it just Daniel who has done this to me? she wondered. Daniel and my own hopeless feelings for him?

But it was three more weeks before she stumbled on the right answer to the question.

CHAPTER TEN

'HI!' SAID a friendly voice just beyond the high laminated bench that surrounded the nurses' station. Rosalie looked up from some notes and found Cathy Trevalley standing there.

'Well, hello stranger!' she said, genuinely pleased to see the young doctor. 'My goodness, don't tell me you've finished your stint in the wilds of Wales already! Has time gone that quickly?'

'It has, hasn't it?' Cathy agreed. 'Yes, the locum is finished, but I've got a permanent place at another partnership near there that's actually nicer.'

'Congratulations!'

'Thanks!' She flushed a little and Rosalie noted the fact but didn't pay it much attention. She had been feeling tired all morning and was now battling a queasiness that was becoming familiar. If she had to speak in the next few seconds, she thought, something terribly messy and unpleasant would probably happen.

I must go to the doctor, she decided. This has been going on for weeks now, and it's getting worse! Could it be mononucleosis?

But Cathy was still speaking. 'I've just had lunch with Daniel down the road,' she said. 'So I thought I'd drop in. Dad doesn't know I'm arriving today, and I'm hoping I can book him for dinner. Is he around?'

'Not at the moment,' Rosalie said. Her nausea had subsided now. It seemed to come and go unpredictably, which was another feature of this mysterious ailment. Quite possibly when she *did* go to the doctor she'd be feeling quite well and would have no symptoms to describe at all! It was one of the reasons she had been putting off making an appointment. 'Your father had surgery all morning,' she informed Cathy now. 'He's probably at lunch somewhere, then he'll be in here later. Will you wait?'

'No, I don't think so,' the younger woman said. 'To tell you the truth, I'm a bit nervous about seeing him. You see, I've got some news that will probably set his hair on fire. I'm engaged!'

'Oh. . .' It was Daniel. It had to be Daniel. That was her only thought, and for several moments she could not even summon enough equilibrium to congratulate Cathy, even though politeness, not to mention friendship, demanded it. Then she saw that the younger woman was looking at her strangely. . .and sympathetically.

'His name is Alec McGowan,' Cathy said quickly and clearly. 'He's a vet. . . Scottish. You wouldn't know him.'

'Alec McGowan. . .' Rosalie echoed blankly. 'Congratulations, Cathy. . .'

Not Daniel at all. And it was obvious that Cathy had guessed the secret of her own feelings about the cardiologist. But nothing was said openly by either of them, and that was a relief. Instead, tactfully and blessedly, Cathy went on talking about her own personal life and Rosalie pushed aside the hopeless situation to enjoy Cathy's evident happiness.

'I've known him for ages,' the new general practitioner was saying. 'But it took him a long time to realise that I was throwing myself at him.' She laughed. 'He persisted in being just good friends until I had to wangle my way into that locum job in Llandovery and practically camp on his doorstep.'

'He lives near there?'

'Yes, in Llandilo. One of your patients a couple of months ago was from that area. The Towy Valley.'

'Mr Powys! Of course!' The Welshman had had a successful transplant but was still up in the isolation annexe in CICU.

'Alec has bought into a veterinary practice there and wants to stay. . .and so do I. I love it! Cardiology has lost me, I'm afraid. . .and I'm afraid to tell Dad.'

'Cardiology never had a chance, did it?' Rosalie teased.

'Neither did Daniel Canaday, although I know Dad would have liked a specialist son-in-law almost as much as a specialist daughter.' Carefully she did not look at Rosalie as she spoke.

'Your father will get over it,' Rosalie managed.

'I know, and I've prepared him as well as I could. Didn't dare to be too specific about Alec, though, in case it fell through. I'm so happy it didn't!'

'So am I,' Rosalie said sincerely. 'You really look sparkling when you mention his name.'

'Do I?' the young doctor smiled. 'Yes, I *feel* sparkling. . . Well, I won't wait for Dad. . .'

She paused. It was two o'clock now, and people were arriving for the afternoon visiting hour. A blond man in his late thirties with a significant pot-belly had just thrust his way up to the desk, carrying a big newspaper-wrapped parcel of half-eaten chips, slathered in tomato sauce, vinegar and salt.

'I'm here to see my Dad,' he said. 'Kevin Mellish. Can I throw these away somewhere?'

'I'll take them,' Rosalie offered gallantly, seizing the soggy parcel. 'Your father is in bed sixteen.'

He turned with a curt nod at just the right moment, while Rosalie had taken a breath at the *wrong* one. Her nostrils were filled with the strong smell of the greasy chips and their gluggy condiments and they had given her such instant nausea that she had to throw the parcel quickly into the nearest bin and fight for control.

'Tell him I dropped by, and that I'll see him at home,' Cathy was saying, picking up her bag and unaware that anything was amiss. 'And ask him to put aside the evening for me if he can.'

'Mm-hmm,' Rosalie nodded, hoping desperately that the surgeon's daughter would leave before disaster struck.

Fortunately, on a cheery call, of 'Bye!' she did.

Rosalie sank into a chair as far from the bin and its offending contents as she could get, breathing deeply and carefully until her nausea subsided. The pot-bellied visitor had gone, Cathy had gone, and she was blessedly alone at last.

What is *wrong* with me? she wondered feverishly. Perhaps it's something really serious. A bowel blockage. . . Lupus. . .

Her medical training suggested half a dozen lurid and ghastly possibilities, and she knew she was in danger of panicking seriously. Trying to stay calm, she ran through the list of symptoms she had experienced for several weeks now. Fatigue, nausea, a bloated, crampy feeling at times, an odd sensitivity to smells and tastes that she normally didn't mind. . .

And suddenly it clicked, as an image of Kevin Mellish's son's protruding belly came to her again. She had often thought to herself how unattractive a man was when he looked as if he were. . . Pregnant! I'm pregnant! It had to be impossible, and at the same time it had to be true. She calculated one or two vital dates, realised that the regular rhythm of her cycle was thoroughly out of order, remembered certain chapters from nursing textbooks, and was quite sure.

For the hour of work that remained her reaction to the idea was simply numbness. Something she had long since believed could never happen to her was, quite suddenly and inexplicably, happening.

Jackie Billings bounced up to the desk for a chat. 'My brothers have been at it again,' she began, clearly very proud of her two new stepbrothers and their mischievous antics.

With her new heart in place and beating strongly, and the immunosuppressant drug Cyclosporin doing its work to prevent her body from rejecting the organ, she looked like a different person. Some of the premature adulthood of her manner had been replaced by a childish vibrancy now, and her blue eyes sparkled in a pixie face that had lost its grey aura of fatigue.

The heart biopsy that Daniel Canaday had performed last week, snaking a thin instrument through a vein in her neck to extract minute pieces of heart tissue for examination and analysis, had shown none of the tell-tale signs of rejection, and in a few more days she would be discharged.

Rosalie listened patiently to the young girl's anecdote about her stepbrothers and responded with enough amusement to please Jackie, but she was relieved when Mrs Rogerson arrived to distract her daughter. Only another half-hour till she could think properly. . .

Mechanically, she answered visitors' questions and instructed her new junior in a basic procedure. Hazily, she gave Cathy's message to Howard and had a quick chat with him, the contents of which she could afterwards remember not a word. Absently, she reported to the incoming staff on the events of the day. Frowningly, she got into her car and thought, I must stop at a chemist. Those new pregnancy test kits that you can do at any time of the day. . . I think they're quite reliable. . .

She drove out of the way of her usual route home, not wanting to stop at Latham's Pharmacy, where she was known quite well. Instead, she went to a big, anonymous chain pharmacy but, even so, the small cardboard box that she brought to the cash register might have had bells attached, so conscious was she of what it contained.

At home, with her long experience of nursing, she found the instructions easy to understand and carry out, and fifteen minutes later she had the result. It was, as she knew it would be, positive.

And then reaction set in. Against all reason, she was
ecstatic. The secret sorrow she had carried with her all
these years had been wiped away, and she already felt
a brooding desire to cocoon herself away and dream
of tender, dimpled skin, fat little hands splashing in a
bath, gurgles of laughter, and even the tender duty of
waking in the night to answer a helpless creature's
cries.

The possibility of not continuing with the pregnancy
or of not keeping the child never entered her mind.
There were plenty of single mothers around these
days. She would manage, somehow, and she would
not be ashamed. . .

Only then did she really think of Daniel, and it
brought a sudden stab of such pain to her that for
several minutes her happiness about the baby was
quite gone.

Most people would think I was a fool, she realised.
Having a baby by the man isn't going to help me get
over loving him! She would have to tell him! He has a
right to know. . .and a right to see the child if he wants
to, and to claim it as his.

If he wanted to. That was the crunch, of course.
Very possibly he would want nothing to do with the
baby, particularly as it would mean ongoing contact
with Rosalie herself down the years. At that thought,
she was tempted not to tell him, but after struggling
with the idea she knew that she had to do it soon. . .
today.

In fact, *now*! Get it over with, get the thing settled,
give him a chance to decide what he wanted so that
she could get on with her own plans, get the ordeal of
seeing him—and loving him even more now that he
had done *this* to her—safely out of the way.

Hurrying inside, she pulled off her uniform and
rummaged in the wardrobe for something to put on.
She found the dress she had worn months ago when
she had gone to the ballet with Daniel. Its royal purple

was bold and cheering, and it had a warm memory attached. Not caring that it might be too dressy for the unique thing she was about to do, Rosalie put it on. She needed to feel attractive for this interview with Daniel.

I should ring him, ask him if it's all right to come over, she thought, and she dialled the number — which she had memorised weeks ago like a foolish school-girl — without stopping to think.

'Hello?' It was his voice, after only one ring, and she found at once that she couldn't speak, dropping the receiver back into its cradle as her heart pounded.

I'll just go there, she decided. It'll be easier in person.

Not allowing herself to think about or plan the interview, she got into the car and drove, having to consult the map twice in her distracted state. He answered her ring at his bell immediately, frowned when he saw her in her magnificently simple purple, and drew her wordlessly into the house. He was brewing coffee, had his shirt-sleeves rolled up to reveal powerful forearms, and must only have just got home from the hospital when he had answered the phone twenty minutes ago, Rosalie realised.

'Sit down,' he said, indicating a brown leather director's chair — one of a set of four that were grouped around the smooth-topped wooden kitchen table. 'This is a surprise.' He was still frowning. She hugged nervous arms around herself defensively, and wished that, after all, she had worn baggy trousers and a nondescript blouse. Why did his gaze always make her feel so very female? 'Coffee?' He held out the fresh, steaming brew.

She had considered small talk, but now events overtook her and made a subtle beginning impossible. The smell of the coffee, usually so fragrant and appe-tising to her, had produced the familiar nausea again and as she fought for it to subside the words came falling out of themselves. 'I'm pregnant.'

He didn't pretend to any confusion, and said slowly after a shocked pause, 'I thought you were. . .taking precautions. I shouldn't have assumed it. I'm sorry.'

'Precautions?' She laughed and suddenly tears glistened on her lashes as she got restlessly to her feet. 'Oh, if only you knew! I thought I couldn't have children. Mike and I tried for four years. I'm so *happy*!' Her voice broke and, blinded by tears, she felt his arms come around her, warm and soft through the giving fabric of her dress.

'Happy?' he whispered. 'Rosalie! Do you know what you're saying?'

'Yes.' She fought to regain control and pulled away. This was no time to be crying. Still less was it time to be cherishing the touch of him against her. She continued, her chin raised firmly, 'I'm going to keep the baby, but don't worry. I won't ask anything from you that you don't want to give. It's completely up to you. That's why I wanted to tell you as soon as possible. To give you time to think. You needn't acknowledge the child as yours at all. . .or we can come to some definite practical arrangement about. . .visitation. That's what it's called, isn't it?' She looked up and forced herself to meet his gaze, wanting to show her good intentions in her face.

But he stepped back, his eyes narrowed and his shoulders wary and stiff. 'Let's get this straight,' he said. 'You're only telling me because I have a. . .how shall we put it?. . .biological right to know.' He was furiously angry, she saw with a sudden *frisson* of doubt and fear.

'I suppose you could phrase it like ——'

He didn't let her finish. 'And I'm to be generously allowed visiting rights to the child if I want them. It's as if we'd both been left a share in a piece of property in someone's will. Is that how you really see it? A weekend for you, a weekend for me, and if we manage things properly we can probably pick the baby up from child-care each week, like collecting a key from under a flowerpot and we need never see each other at all. Don't you want to even consider the possibility that this baby might bring us together, and it *ought* to bring us together, that we might get married. . .?'

'Married?'

'Yes! Married! People do, occasionally, you know.'

Rosalie was so shocked that she blurted the truth, standing like an island of pure emotion in the middle of the room. 'I would, oh, I would marry you tomorrow if you loved me, but just as a way for us both to have the child — '

'What do you mean, *if* I loved you?' He had crossed the space that separated them and seized her wrists in a painful grip, before sliding his hands hotly up her arms. '*If* I loved you,' he repeated scornfully. 'Of course I love you, damn it! What have we been fighting over and agonising over these past months if not the fact that I love you but you can't give yourself to it? You hold back, you mistrust it, you don't feel it enough yourself. . . I don't know what it is. All I know is that it has been damned painful for both of us and now you talk about "*if* I loved you", as though *that* was the missing link.'

'You mean. . .? What do you mean?' she stammered, bewildered by his anger and by the meaning of his words. 'Then you *do* love me? Then. . .then you want to marry me because you love me?'

And suddenly he was close to her, holding her, whispering in her ear. 'Yes, *yes*, Rosalie! Don't tell me *that's* what you've doubted all along, that's what has been holding you back?'

'You never *said* it,' she murmured helplessly. 'I thought — '

'Didn't I *show* it,' though? I thought I showed it in

a dozen ways. Wanting to be with you whenever I could, scarcely able to keep my hands off you. . .'

'But that was wanting, not love. That was the problem. I thought you wanted an affair. You never said otherwise. I thought that a man of thirty-two. . . and me, at thirty-seven, thinking I could never give you children even if by some miracle your physical desire *did* last and turn into something deeper. . . although I couldn't believe that it would,' she cried incoherently. 'Why did you never say it?'

'The moment was never right,' he answered, as helpless as she was now. 'I didn't want to say it in the heat of passion. I wanted to say it in some softer mood, but at those times I could always sense your misgivings. I still can't believe this — that that was what you were waiting to hear. I wanted to spend more time together — to spend *all* our time together, in bed and out of it, so that we both knew it deep in our bones, so that we had both said it in hundreds of ways without words before we sealed it *with* them. Words are so weak, sometimes, compared with this. . .'

His lips grazed her throat, then travelled upwards to her mouth, taking it in a kiss that was searing and tender, hungry and very, very long. Finally he pulled away. 'And why did you think I only wanted an affair? Because of this ridiculous thing about our ages! Can't I get it into your head that you're astonishingly beautiful to me, and you always will be, ripely, richly beautiful in a way that. . . I don't know. . .little Elise Jones won't be for another twenty years, if ever? And you're astonishingly *young* to me, too, and you always will be, the way your laughter is so fresh, the way you touch your flowers and drink in their beauty and scent . . .it's ageless. So, please, once and for all, can we *forget* that I'm "younger" than you?'

'Yes, Daniel,' she answered meekly, her face pressed into his shoulder. It felt so right, and it *was* ageless. He gave her just the same joys as he had described — a sense of freshness, of newness, of life.

'And can you remember that I love you utterly, and want to marry you and be with you and have our baby and. . .pluck the richness of this thing to its very depths, Rosalie?' he finished, more serious and solemn than she had ever seen him, as he ran the tips of his fingers lightly along her jaw, setting every nerve-ending on fire.

'Yes. . .'

'Now, do you want some coffee, while we talk this thing out thoroughly?'

'No. . .'

'No?'

'It makes me feel so sick.'

He laughed, a deep, full sound, and tossed back his head. The gesture made him look so wild and strong that it reminded her of something he had once said, and she went to him timidly, needing his touch again. 'Daniel, you said once that you weren't a particularly civilised person. Don't you think that gave me grounds for thinking that you weren't the marrying kind?'

'Not at all,' he growled, running his hands hungrily and possessively over her fullest curves. 'The kind of marriage I envisage isn't a particularly civilised institution.'

'What kind of marriage *do* you envisage?'

'An elopement, for a start.'

'An elopement?'

'Yes. Do you really want to stand around in a veil with a lot of distant relations that you haven't seen for twenty years looking on?'

'No, but——'

'And since gossip is going to insist anyway — and I don't give a damn! — that we only got married because of the baby, why don't we cut the pretence. . .get married next week. . .wangle some leave. . .go to Paris. . .or Spain?'

'Spain?'

'Turkey?'

'Paris *and* Turkey,' she laughed. 'For romance and adventure.'

'Actually, I don't think I'll have coffee either,' he mused now. 'I rather think I'd like to go and sit somewhere more comfortable, don't you?'

'Mm-hmm. . .'

'My bed is very nice. . .'

A long time later, she confessed, 'I thought you might have been falling for Cathy Trevalley.'

'Cathy?'

'She's a delightful person.'

'She is,' he acknowledged. 'And good luck to her vet!'

'Oh, you know about that.'

'She invited me to lunch especially to tell me. In fact, I'd suspected for a while. We had dinner together that week she spent at the hospital, and she told me she knew exactly what her father was trying to do with the two of us. She was quite open about it, and quite adamant that it wouldn't work. Nothing personal, she insisted, and I guessed that there was a man involved somewhere. Then she asked about you and Howard, and whether I thought it was serious. I said I didn't know, I didn't take any notice of your personal affairs because they were none of my business. I don't think she believed me. I was feeling pretty sore about you that week, and it showed.'

'Yes,' Rosalie answered thoughtfully. 'Today she was very anxious to let me know that it wasn't you she was engaged to. She knew how I felt. Do you think everyone does?'

'No. Strange, really, isn't it? There's definitely a rainbow over everything, but apparently no one else can see it!'

They laughed. . .and kissed. Later still, she asked, 'If we just have this one child, will it matter to you?'

'Not a bit. We'll take it as it comes. But why should we have just the one child?'

'Well, it seems rather a fluke that I've managed to get pregnant at all, when Mike and I tried for so long.'

'Did you have any tests done back then?'

'No, we didn't. I was just about to when he died. But for a long time I just assumed. . .and Mike did too. . .that it was no good. That if I was infertile, nothing could be done. I know now that women can take——'

'But why assume that it was you?' he whispered.

'You mean. . .'

'It was probably Mike. Evidence points to that now, doesn't it? You and I are probably as fertile as frogs.'

'*Frogs*?'

'And we'll have ten children by the turn of the century if we're not careful.'

'I don't know about ten,' she said, 'But. . .will a baby fit into this flat?'

'This flat? No! But we won't be living here.'

'At my cottage, then. . .'

'Darling Rosalie?'

'Yes?'

'What about somewhere new that we've found together?'

A vision rose in her mind's eye of the time they would spend together looking for a place to live that fitted them both and she knew he was right. This was the start of something important. No more fears and memories of the past to cloud what happened between them. A new life. . .together. . .and as they turned into each other's arms once more on this now tumbled bed she knew that this life had already started.